THE MORGAINE CYCLE ONE:

Gwyliwr

Zane Newitt

Text copyright © Zane Newitt 2022
Design copyright © Chrissie Yeomans 2022
All rights reserved.

Zane Newitt has asserted his right under the Copyright, Designs and Patents Act 1988 to be identified as the author of this work.

No part of this book may be reprinted or reproduced or utilised in any form or by electronic, mechanical or any other means, now known or hereafter invented, including photocopying or recording, or in any information storage or retrieval system, without the permission in writing from the Publisher and Author.

This title is intended for the enjoyment of adults, and is not recommended for children due to the mature content it contains.

This book is meant to be educational, informative and entertaining. Although the author and publisher have made every effort to ensure that the information in this book was correct at the time of publication, the author and publisher do not assume and hereby disclaim any liability to any party for loss, damage or disruption caused by errors or omissions, whether such errors or omissions result from negligence, accident or any other cause.

First published 2022
by Rowanvale Books Ltd
The Gate
Keppoch Street
Roath
Cardiff
CF24 3JW
www.rowanvalebooks.com

A CIP catalogue record for this book is available from the British Library.
ISBN: 978-1-914422-05-8
Hardback ISBN: 978-1-914422-07-2

Acknowledgements

Delving into antediluvian issues is fascinating, fun and complicated ground.

Although the Morgaine Cycle is written from a biblical, henotheistic worldview, every culture and every religion share a similar framework, a skeletal outline of the same mysterious history:
- Visitors came from the sky, or sometimes from 'the northern country.'
- These Otherworldly Beings, be they labeled as aliens, angels or gods, interbred with humans.
- The offspring included giants, demigods and an array of fairy-like creatures.
- The resulting civilization was very advanced, prosperous and just – for a time.
- The gods became increasingly violent, bloodthirsty and corrupt.
- There was a small remnant of mortals whose bloodlines were not poisoned by the Sky People.
- A higher authority (a One True God, a higher council of deities, etc.) sent a great Flood to destroy the gods, and most of mankind as well, sparing very few faithful in order to start civilization anew.

This simple sketch becomes a myriad of questions and ponderings, all of which have serious worldview implications, none of which can, or should, be taken dogmatically.
- Why does God give angels, who are not made to marry, reproductive parts?
- Did the angels actually have sexual intercourse with women? Or was it DNA/gene-splicing or another method that brought their 'sky children' into being?
- What was the population before the Flood?
- Was there a 'pre-Flood' Greek civilization? Sumerian?
- Why did God change lifespans from nine hundred to one hundred and twenty, then to eighty years?
- Are the faeries spirits? Corporal? Or both?

- What is the real shape and construct of the universe? All of the ancients agree on a model, and none of those models agree with NASA.
- How did the Nephilim return after the Flood?
  - Another incursion?
  - Noah's daughters-in-law?
  - Did some of the Nephilim survive the Flood?
  - Other?
- Are there Nephilim today?

These are the questions that my son, Avery Newitt, and I ask, betwixt and between enjoying football, baseball and the occasional pint of beer or cider. I truly appreciate that we have had, from his youth, a shared interest in pursuit of the truth of 'where we come from, why we are here, and where we are going.' My son is a pure worldview deconstructionist, ever seeking to line things up, break them down, and study them from a thousand angles. His insight, ideas and curiosity have resulted in a number of rewrites, and a lot of growth in my understanding of this vast subject.

For example, you can't have Zeus as the God of Thunder, slinging lightning bolts, before the existence of rain. Thus, he was the God of the Air, enjoying the perfect mists of the antediluvian world, in his career before the Flood, the later attributes having to, by necessity and logic, come after.

Avery has helped me clean up and purify so many topics like this over the years, just by virtue of dialoguing, pondering and thinking through the matter of the old gods in light of a Scriptural Worldview. This is no easy task, and impossible without his support!

This book is dedicated to you, Avery!

Love – Dad.

Table of Contents

Chapter 1
Before Merlin Was...   11

Chapter 2
The First Goddess was a Woman   20

Chapter 3
The Primal Witch   24

Chapter 4
The Girl with Cloven Hooves   34

Chapter 5
The First Murder   40

Chapter 6
The Consort of Satan   45

Chapter 7
The Bird Has Flown the Coop   53

Chapter 8
The Days of Jared   62

Chapter 9
A Second Fall   66

Chapter 10
Atlantis   72

Chapter 11
Men Are the Problem   75

Chapter 12
"Show Them"   81

Chapter 13
Women are the Problem   90

Chapter 14
Fire and Water   97

Chapter 15
No Place for Them   104

Chapter 16
Stacking Ghosts — 107

Chapter 17
Britain Before the Flood — 113

Chapter 18
Go to Her — 115

Chapter 19
Become Their Accusation — 123

Chapter 20
Lilith Versus the Archangel Uriel — 128

Chapter 21
The Nursemaid — 133

Chapter 22
The King of the Tylwyth Teg — 137

Chapter 23
God Intervenes
The Shining One and the Hermit — 142

Chapter 24
The Owl and the Raven — 147

Chapter 25
The Passing of Eve — 152

Chapter 26
The Wages of Plotting — 158

Chapter 27
A Short Marriage to a Tall Girl — 162

Chapter 28
Lilith Versus the Morrigan — 167

Chapter 29
Of Schemes and Plots; of Freakish Monsters and Crossbreeds; of the Fall of Atlantis — 171

Chapter 30
What the Devil Means for Evil, God Uses for Good — 175

Morgana, Morgana, M... ... ...

Chapter 1
Before Merlin Was

Broceliande Forest
525 A.D.

When the screech owl wails, 'tis usually in celebration that someone or something has perished and a feast is nigh.

But this certain winged trumpet, so appalled at the terror witnessed below her circuits, looses rather a wailing of warning: a desperate signal for men to harken, and to stay away.

She protests into the summer night, swooping low o'er the face of a large, still lake that sprawls as the forearm of a mighty woodsman, his veins dispensing into a myriad of labyrinth-like streams that give drink and passage to the diverse creaturekind – and 'otherkind' – that dwells within the gargantuan Enchanted Wood of the Bretons.

She bawls at the waters, she screams at the trees; she screeches a shriek of trembling over the harsh judgement she hath beheld in her nighttime flights. The screech owl climbs then descends again, spiraling her loud dance of admonition over the glassy body of water, hoping that its mistresses might hear her, and turn away the bewitched.

The lake is named, after the seven who dwell there, *The Faeries' Mirror*.

Motionless, it presents as a great blue looking-glass by day, the black marble of a great hall by night. It is as a crystal cage for the Korrigan sirens smiling in illuminated abeyance, flowing, twirling and turning in their shimmering gowns of white and samite just beneath its surface. To the clear ceiling of their glass house they ascend, the seductive allure of their visage ensnaring many a lad who cannot help but to peer close, closer, and yet closer again, forgetting that the water *is* *water* and no glass at all, and suffer the fall.

The calm is a trap, The Faeries' Mirror a snare.

But not of death; these water sprites are for mischief, not for malice. After overcoming the fright of drowning and at last yielding in their vain struggle to grapple with the Fair Folk, the knight, farmer or priest (for these Korrigan are no respecters of men when it comes to their revelries) is raptured away to the worlds beneath the lake and there treated to feasting, to dance, to play. They are titillated by riddles and puffed up by tales of dragon and lance and then, once the special herbs in the mead and cider have their aims accomplished, introduced to lovemaking unprecedented and of no comparison to what can be enjoyed amongst the world of men and their mortal women.

And in the convalescence of happy recovery, when all fluids are spent, with the gateway to a man's soul most open, will the Korrigan cast her spell.

Never to strike the Fae. And for sure not thrice. Always, without fail, to leave them their best milk, butter or barley. Never to harm a beast or mistreat a child (for a changeling might be hosted and reared unawares). But the penalties for breaking these are none too harsh and the consequences not severe. Merely to wander in another realm for three-score three hundred years whilst loved ones back in Llwdaw or Cymru age and pass away, or to lose virility and suffer young the thinning of the hair or graying of the crown, is the most severe of it. For these faeries hail from the Good Court; their custom is to play and harass Man in benevolence, elsewise to help him at times per their ancient and peculiar laws and ways.

The screech owl screams a scream of begging to the Seven Korrigan, that they might aid her and the whole of the wood tonight in turning men away before they approach the mouth of the lake. For the joyous revelries of frolicking with sensual spirits notwithstanding, the pond and its veins pour into a valley where dwells a faerie not so benevolent, neither gracious to the flaws, misgivings and naughtiness of men.

Within the vastness of Broceliande, just beyond The Faeries' Mirror, where the streams run and sprawl, then come again once more into confluence, opens the mouth of **The Valley of No Return**, where dwells the Punisher of Love Falsely So-Called.

And on this summer night in the land of the Bretons, the screech owl cries and cries, for yet another knight has come. *And this one with a special, regal walk.*

Lured. Lured across a great distance and quite in a trance he treads, his steed following the direction of a great stag.

From Caerleon in Cymru he comes. Not unto wanton play; rather unto risk of gruesome death.

And the playful faeries hear neither owl nor ghost, neither watchman nor guard, for each of the Seven are presently preoccupied with three other lads not yet twenty, splashing and giggling beneath the twinkling lights, making sloppy and sticky love under the summer stars.

But moreover, the Korrigan could in no wise help the knight anyhow, as the Seven are no match for the One. Indeed, neither could seventy, nor seventy times seventy.

***

The witch's familiar, a warty crested newt specked with black spots, returned in advance of the knight it had poisoned, but the witch, of odd disposition and disinterested temperament, took no joy in seeing the creeping thing.

She sat upon a throne constructed of thigh bones bound by metal twine. Although she made her bed and ate her meals in a nearby pavilion (where also spread upon a great round table lay diverse and cruel killing instruments), the Punisher sat oft on her throne, staring upon her scrying bowl: a great basin that rested upon a singular gray and cracked pillar. There within her tower made of skulls grayed with wattle and daub, she would watch the bowl and, using her Sight, anticipate the arrival of the accused.

On this particular night, the listless goddess had little interest in adding another brain-pan to the architecture. The quantity of the sins of men disturbed her as she made a visual census of the fortress her killing had wrought.

"*One* unfaithful man ruins the life of his spouse, devastates and forever alters the course of life for their children, disrupts his place of labor, divides friends, destroys lives. One!" she hollered to no one in particular.

The witch was slight, and her feet dangled above the moist gray rocks that served as the floor of the tomb-like chamber where she brooded. Shifting and delivering an emotional kick that crackled the thigh bones repurposed as her seat cushion, she continued, "If but one adulterer ruins a score of lives, what of the seven hundred deceased offenders I see before me?"

She gracefully leapt from her throne, knelt, and permitted the newt to crawl into her hand and rest upon her shoulder.

She was adorned in a gray garment, which was a singular leather piece that spanned from her chin to her toes. The image of a spider, sewn with a thousand tiny interlocking and alternating leather scales and plated with a bright red hourglass pattern made of rubies, served as the breastplate. Whether the eight legs that formed her cape were decorative or real and demonic is lost to the shadow of legend.

Her hair was braided with countless rows of gray threaded beads, a few hundred of which served as partial curtains over her large, bronze-gold eyes. In every particular, she was as a black widow perched in the midst of a tower of doom. And presently, another accused approached.

Her custom was to give them no place for defense, no adjudication or procedure. Rather, her words were constant and unchanging. Her mind's eye would see Mordred betraying the Great Pendragon by the Harlot Queen Gwenhwyfar, and she would charge the proxy victim before her: "How would your spouse feel?"

Typically, the unfaithful would have about thirty seconds to ponder the Executioner's encouragements of empathy ere his spirit was removed from his body, which was added to the stack of bones. But on this particular sultry night, the witch had grown melancholy, bored, and somewhat sickened by the thing she had become.

Has my purging the world of so many sinners undone what I have seen? Filled the abyss in my heart cankered by the treachery of my own son? In no wise. Would the Summer Kingdom not be better on balance had I slain him, and not these seven hundred flawed fathers, husbands, warriors, farmers, artisans and priests?

And now does a young knight approach the same age as my son. As my Mordred.

The guiding stag was the Gaulish god Cernunnos. The Spider had captured him prancing about Broceliande, turning leaves green before their time and spreading merriment to pixies. This disagreed with the witch, so she had placed him unwillingly under her employ that he might toil instead of frolic.

The old god trotted into the arched doorway of her tower, head down, huffing and snorting protests of fatigue, the beast's eyes saying, *Here, another one if you must.*

And behind him, behold the handsome knight with curly black locks and blue eyes, decorated in the colors and sigils of Lyonesse, sitting stiff as a statue upon his steed. The long trip, which had included Roman roads, wild fields and a ferry boat, had not wrested him from his deep trance.

The familiar spirit wearing the newt's flesh had whispered enchantments and incantations into the ear of the unfaithful lover for the whole of the previous night, when he and a lass had been caught in the very act, their activities intensified by the poisons contained in the mucus of the salamander.

"Awaken," commanded the Punishing Spider calmly. In her single word did the poison vanish and the statuesque boy animate.

He possessed a quiet bravery coupled with reservation regarding the matter, and the ends of the matter. The hot *night of irony* continued as the witch, who at last fancied a conversation, waited patiently for a young man who accepted his sentence and offered nothing but a guilty and reverent gaze to the floor below.

In petulance at his respect and silence, the slight fae became something *taller.*

The knight could not help but change the panning of his eyes from the floor and her feet to her face and the ceiling. Dust and not a few small stones were displaced where the crown of her beaded head breached the top of the tower and, in the eyes of the young man, the height of the firmament as well. His jaw dropped and his knees knocked uncontrollably, knuckles shaking out of their joints.

Cernunnos scurried into the night, wanting none of the witch in this form (for the day-to-day version was dread enough for both men and gods), leaving the knight to meet his fate alone.

The witch stooped, meeting the young man's eyes, and by her iron will compelled him to speak.

"Lyonesse," she started. "You are from here, yet you were caught in your untoward deed in the south of Cymru. Ironic that you cannot outrun your sins across the Channel, and that you have been brought home to die!"

"It was a sin of numbing, a fornication of forgetting, for I am undone by forbidden love, and death would free me most welcomely of the grievous wound upon my heart."

The witch was instantly three-and-one-half shoe-lengths of an average man yet again. "You have a story, and are not just another married lecher taking a maiden in a field."

The goddess again made summation in her mind's eye of her long years as a *bone collector*, as she hid from her office, her duty, her children and her true home. Perhaps this young man, whom she instantly fancied for the strength of his vulnerability, might help her break the spell; the spell of trauma cast upon herself.

"What are you called?" she continued.

"Amongst the Bretons, I am called Guiomar, and to the Cymry, Gryngamawr," he responded.

The witch liked him.

She liked his name. She liked his countenance.

Through the workings of her dark powers, cider and lamb didst appear and he did eat; only not in the tower of bones, for she bade him come to lodgings in her pavilion.

When he was rested and fed, she asked Guiomar to tell her how that he had become an adulterer.

"I have an aunt in the kingdom of Lyonesse. And though she be aunt, we are similar in age. Against my will and nature did I fall in love with her. An unholy, unnatural love."

Guiomar's voice broke as he spoke these things, and the Spider could tell that the young man did suffer a *real* broken heart, and did indeed welcome death.

"In the flower of youth, did she dally with you or gestate these feelings?"

"Nay. She is the most temperate, kind and moral woman—"

The witch (being also a mother of young men) offered an attempt at humor. "She sounds dreadfully dull."

Guiomar cracked the smallest of smiles. "Not dull. A warm woman with the sense of her own office and destiny."

"You love her so." The Spider's memories rushed to Llaniltud Fawr and the great love of her youth.

"Forever," he responded.

The punisher of untrue men embraced the untrue man, holding and comforting him.

"Was this love cruelly unrequited?" she enquired.

"It was kindly and graciously unrequited, for no part of her can be cruel."

"That's even worse!"

This time he laughed, and then they cried at her musing.

"Her father, seeing my fancy, did protect her virtue and cause me to marry another. Doing the deeds of the marital bedroom broke me and I abandoned my young wife and went to Caerleon, where I could hurl my every occupation into the life of service at arms." Guiomar searched the night for the remaining words, a deep embarrassment overtaking him, such that he turned ghostly white. "I… served the High King!"

Hearing mention of the Bear of Glamorgan caused the witch's eyes to well, and her intuition told her the story was about to take a disastrous turn.

"And then I betrayed my king!" The knight openly wept.

How can I slay you, young sir? For I, too, have betrayed him.

"The queen saw me at the games a fortnight ago, exchanging swordplay with the heroes Gwalchmai and Gareth."

"Two of the very best," she proudly inserted.

"She did create a ruse and situation whereby she could ensure we were alone, and the woman I lay with was none other than Queen Gwenhwyfar herself."

The witch did not give a reactive or judgmental response. She was only moderately shocked that she had not seen clearly in the scrying basin the woman involved in the act. For if she had, she would have had mercy and not condemnation for the lad. And she, having the benefit of *history* with this whore, did have mercy now.

Far from killing the knight, she consoled his sobbing and offered, "She is a skilled and practiced seductress, a far more lethal siren than the sprites that dance and tease over there at the lake. You were over-matched from the start, innocent and sweet Guiomar."

How many other men did I slay whose lives were gray and not black? Have I lost all balance between personal responsibility and the reality of our circumstantial, fallen natures?

"She is all of those things, but there is a deeper, more perverse reason I did fornicate with her." He wanted to confess the matter, and the witch's disposition gave him the comfort to have it out of his soul once and for all. "She shares the name of the woman I loved, and it empowered me to cry out the name, enjoying it upon my lips in the motions of our sin. For a few minutes in a heavy and cursed life, I could cry out—"

"Gwenhwyfar," the witch interrupted.

"Aye. My aunt is Gwenhwyfar ferch Gwythyr ap Greidawl. My forbidden love is the Lady of Lyonesse herself."

The Punisher of False Lovers, the Spider of Broceliande, the Dark Witch of the Valley of No Return, had no words herself. She dropped her arms and at last exclaimed, "Ours is the language of heaven; why do we have so few names for our women?" She laughed and laughed, but the laughter was paired with streaming tears.

Guiomar did not understand the meaning or direction of her discourse and looked bewildered, though he tried to laugh with her just the same.

"You are not the first honorable, handsome and true young man to be bewitched nigh unto ruin by TWO GWENHWYFARS!" Here did the Spider unthread her hair dramatically, hundreds of beads as baby spiders scurrying this way and that way across the floor. She rent the breastplate from her garb, exclaiming, "In fact… a similar fate befell my own brother." Now it was she who was confessing.

"Your brother?" The knight had not discovered the meaning, nor the matter.

"Fear not." She clasped his hand in a maternal, protective clamp. "My brother is the man you betrayed."

"This cannot be. They say the Spider of the Valley of No Return is thousands of years old and not of the daughters of Adam." His tone was a tempest of confusion with no guile.

"You forget what they say about King Arthur's sister," she whispered softly. "How that she is at once just two years his senior but also older than these lands."

"You are—" Guiomar felt as if an invisible dagger would cleave his tongue if he uttered the words. He paused and reversed course, dreading presumption. "Who are you, my merciful lady?"

"A more apropos query would be 'When am I?'" she responded.

She liked Guiomar, and the long years of killing quickly, else being in solitude, had rendered her lonely. She liked him.

And she would tell him her tale.

"When are you, my lady?" he asked as bidden.

The screech owl returned and cried, this time not in warning but in jealous inquisitiveness. The witch acknowledged the bird with an upward glance, then took the knight by the cheeks and spake boldly:

"I am Morgaine of the Faeries, and before even the Merlin was, I am…"

Chapter 2
The First Goddess was a Woman

"For in the resurrection they neither marry, nor are given in marriage, but are as the angels of God in heaven."
Matthew 22:30

The Most High God spoke, and the creation came into being by his Word. Over six days did He fashion the heaven and the earth for a pattern unto Men.

And on the fourth day did the Lord God create the Heavenly Hosts, the luminary beings, and the stars, which are also called angels. The self-same day did He make the Sun to rule the day and the Moon, who was the first being of feminine nature, to rule the night. And she gives her own light.

In this regard was the Moon the first goddess, being subject to the Most High God but more grand in nature than the unique and peculiar beings that God would soon create.

And on the fifth day of creation did the Lord God create three great monsters for to play with, and to demonstrate His power and dominion over the whole of creation. For He alone is God, and the gods cannot stand against Him. By His Word and Wisdom doth He both create and order the world according to the pleasure of His will.

Two of the monsters were sea dragons, and the width of their girth and the length of their tails can no man measure. They were commanded to guard the fountains of the Deep, coiling about the face of the Earth, spending much time in fixed position as two great dams, swallowing their own tails, regulating the waters that circulate in and out of the oceans. These monsters enjoyed free entrance to the waters above the sky, the waters below the sky, and the waters outside the firmament that circumscribe the Earth, the Abyss and the Underworld.

The male dragon was called Leviathan and the female dragon Tiamat.

The Creator God made a third beast: the Behemoth; and to him were given the parts of the world where the dry land appeared.

To these three did the Lord add a great red bird called Ziz, whose wingspan was as a tent cast over the breadth of the sun, so that wherever he flew did the day at once appear as nightfall.

And these four monsters were for the glory and pleasure of the Lord.

Lucifer, the Anointed Cherub, was instantly fond of Tiamat, and though his station was the Throne of Glory, he frequently abandoned his estate for to play with the female dragon. And the Creator God did also play and wrestle with the male dragon.

On the sixth day did God make Man, his special and unique creation. For in the image of God did He fashion Man, meaning:
- The form and likeness of Man is similar to the form and fashion of the manifestation of God.
- Like God, Man is a triune being; his composition includes a soul, a spirit and a body.
- Dominion. Man was made the heir of the Earth, and though the Heavenly Hosts would reign, Man would rule. And the function of the Heavenly Hosts was to teach, support and minister unto Man.

Then Man through rebellion fell, and Death entered the creation.

The Lord God, knowing the ending from the beginning, seeing down the corridor of time that if the sea dragons were to make offspring, no life would be able to stand against them or indeed survive, did by His sovereign will slay Tiamat. And for not this cause only but for an additional future purpose, unknown and not understood by even His most elect angel, did God do this.

Lucifer was forced to see God effortlessly vanquish the angel's consort, dashing each of her seven heads against mountainous stones, the lantern of her eyes casting yellow phosphorescent beacons over ten thousand leagues of water as a cry for help, a moment of despair uncomforted. The beacon faded and the waters were yet hues of blue, purple and in parts ebony again, for Lucifer witnessed God raise His sword, then bring it down fiercely, cleaving her in seven great pieces within the waters.

Lucifer himself, along with seven Watchers (who are elsewhere amongst men called Titans), was made to take the remnants of Tiamat to a special chamber within the Great City, there to salt her flesh for future consumption by the Sons of Adam.

In this regard was Tiamat, like unto the Moon, a primal goddess, though she was but a great beast, and upon Tiamat did Satan's affections rest such that he caused men everywhere to worship the Dragon. And to honor her always in diverse ways.

But in the sense of a Great Goddess, or goddesses, from the beginning of creation there were none directly created by the Most High.

The Cherubs are like unto the beasts of the field, combined with the attributes of Men who are under their charge.

The Seraphim are as fiery serpents, and no angel or man can look upon them.

Thrones are as great glowing wheels wrapped in eyes.

Dominions are as men, save that they have wings.

The Virtues are beings of faint light and subtle form.

Powers are fashioned as sparks of light swirling and twirling in billows of smoke.

Principalities are beings in the form of men, yet made only of a fluid light.

Archangels, like unto Dominions, are in appearance as the princes of men.

Elementals are governed by archangels, and are diverse in their appearance.

Angels are like unto men in every particular, yet having a body of a different glory and lacking the triune nature.

And every angel has a star. And every star is an angel. For a star is the luminary body, the *house made without hands* for a glorious habitation of the Lord. And the Seven Watchers had stars of a different degree of glory than the multitude of other stars that circle the Earth.

God made other heavenly beings besides, for as many are the beasts of the field and fowls of the air, or fish and creatures of the sea and monsters of the Deep, are the diverse kinds of creatures in the heavens.

For God the Creator *is creative.*

But of all the wonderment of the Hosts above, shouting their glory in concert to the Most High, vibrating the cosmos in power, in awe, in grandeur undefined, was there no woman, nor anything like unto woman, neither a forerunner to woman found.

And when God fashioned Eve, the course of history, and reality, changed.

Who possesses such unique beauty that the whole of creaturekind, from the beasts of the fields to the Cherubs above, equally and steadfastly desires her?

For the Moon, though magnificent, did not the Watchers risk all; neither for Tiamat the Dragon did the angels wage war. Rather Eve, and her progeny.

Woman.

And who has wisdom like a daughter of Eve?

The angels can sing and guide men to build a hundred temples, but fall short of what she knows, forgets and then knows again before her first cup of tea.

Who is so close to God that she doth bring forth life and *understand the miracle of it? Lucifer and his legions can but imitate, cross-pollinate and corrupt what already exists; only she can beget something new.*

Wars to be fought over her, rivers of blood to be shed. Fortunes wagered, religions spawned, cruelty formalized, Orders of Conduct chartered. The whole of everything good and bad in the Generations of Men is centered upon Woman.

In this regard was Eve the first goddess, for she is the Mother of all the Living.

And Lilith the Screech Owl was… second.

Chapter 3
The Primal Witch

"¹³ And the Lord God said unto the woman, What is this that thou hast done? And the woman said, The serpent beguiled me, and I did eat.

¹⁴ And the Lord God said unto the serpent, Because thou hast done this, thou art cursed above all cattle, and above every beast of the field; upon thy belly shalt thou go, and dust shalt thou eat all the days of thy life:

¹⁵ And I will put enmity between thee and the woman, and between thy seed and her seed; it shall bruise thy head, and thou shalt bruise his heel."

Genesis 3:13-15

Lucifer, the Light Bearer, the Anointed Cherub, the Son of the Morning. In beauty paramount, save Eve, and in brilliance, unsurpassed.

God had fitted jewels of majesty and musical devices into the very outer covering of the Cherub. Shimmering, sparkling marvel! He was, by his very design, fashioned to pronounce, complement and loudly declare the glory of the Most High.

But now the Light Bearer was *the Dirt Eater.*

From four strong legs to the likeness of a worm did the Lord reduce the Beguiler, and the whole of creaturekind that bore his likeness, to the collective hiss of so many thousand thousand serpents protesting their instant curse and new condition. By His Word did God create the serpent, and by His Word did He condemn it to cracks and crannies and the low places of the Earth.

From the sardius and the topaz to scales and mucus. From diamonds to thistles and thorns. From jasper and emerald to grime and pus.

While yet in the form of the but presently *serpent-cast* (for angels can take on many forms when they traverse below the firmament in the world of men), the rebellious spirit did carefully consider the words of his Creator.

The first prophecy.

"*It*" (her seed) "shall bruise my head?" At first hearing, then still to the fifth or six contemplation, was the utterance as nonsense to the *Helper of Man Turned Adversary* (for God has no adversary, and no equal; 'tis Man in whom the Enemy finds his opponent).

The same Tyrant and Twister of All That is Comely declared that the apes would surely die in the day they partook of the Tree of Knowledge. But they did partake of those grapes, and lo, the day is nearly spent, and Man and Wife yet draw breath.

The Adversary mocks the Lord, but it is a fearful mocking, as a lesser opponent does in the field of battle or at the games, when he overcompensates at finding himself heavily outmatched.

In his heart he mocked. In his head he continued to consider.

Creation had been for one hundred and twenty-nine years, and although Adam had not yet known Eve (for in them was no knowledge of lust, nor any purpose or necessity to continue themselves), Lucifer fully understood that the fowls of the air and the beasts of the field did bring forth life abundantly, reproducing after their own kind.

Emphatically and without exception did *males have seed*, not their mates.

Indeed, when he would manifest in the likeness of a man and walk with Adam upon the Holy Mount (as they had done oft), Lucifer's privy parts did function as a man. Peradventure one day the Creator might indeed make for the angels wives and companions, but there was no indication or inkling of such a purpose, for the whole of the angelic order were as males save the Moon, who was unique in her constitution.

But conceivably (though he had no more desire towards the wife of Adam than would a buffalo lust after a hummingbird), Lucifer surmised that he could beget seed. Or rather – and more easily – if God's prophetic utterance was spiritual or allegorical, Lucifer could bring forth followers and acolytes after his own kind.

Alas, there was no scenario in the boastful and proud mind of the serpent where the Mother of all the Living could do this, for *Eve had no seed*!

Seventy times seven times did the newly Cursed One consider his condemnation, slithering and considering, considering and cursing, as he traversed the Garden, making his way to the twin pillars that were entrance to the Great City.

In his arrogance, the serpent meant to simply slither up to the throne room and engage the Lord about the matter, challenging His words in some manner of grand cosmic debate.

That some kinds of serpents became legless worms had happened in an instant. But beyond this there had been no grand pronouncement, no earthquake, no dramatic appearing of Michael delivering sentence or even accusation on behalf of God. The ethereal dragons that orbited the rafters of heaven yet danced, spiraling and looping, performing against the backdrop of an angelic chorus. And the winged fiery serpents, made so much in the likeness of the Seraph that were their overseers, had befallen no harsh adjudication.

The sky had not fallen, the pillars of the Earth were yet sure, the serpent's head was unscathed, and Adam and Eve surely were still *not dead*.

Gaining confidence, the Scoffer decided to ensure that he *could* take up his original form. The Pondering Schemer rose, and transformed.

He yet shone bright. He was still the Son of the Morning, his brilliance and beauty intact.

Surveying himself – up one arm, slowly and intentionally, and down the next with the same dramatic sequence – the Cherub was filled with greater and growing arrogance, purposing in his heart that he might yet quarrel with his Maker over the but recent events.

And so the Snake stood, and walked, and a cloud of proud light encompassed him.

In the same regard that a kitchen servant has no audience with his king, neither does he that shoes horses sup with the chieftain, the vast majority of angelic beings have never seen and certainly do not know their Creator. They have their roles, responsibilities and place within *His Purpose for the Ages*. He knows and cares for each of them (being omnipresent and omniscient by characteristic), but the reverse is not so; and very, very few angels have approached the Throne of Glory, or spoken personally to God.

But Lucifer has. Lucifer does. And Lucifer purposed to do so again, straightway. For by reason of his original station, he had access.

Direct access.

Proudly, he marched to the gates of the gilded megalopolis, the many-storied pyramid molded of glass and every precious gem. So magnificent was the City that even its outer gates were of spectacular pearl.

God, at this time, walked with Man, and made His home with him. And God's home featured these:
- A pyramid or great mount
- A circle made of stones of fire that measured, calculated and celebrated the movements of the celestial bodies
- A wondrous garden

Eastward through Eden did Satan press until at last he viewed the entrance… of where the City *had been.* And was there no more.

And so the standing Snake fell again to the dust of the earth, his face planted in the rich, cool soils of Paradise, overtaken by shock.

Raising his eyes in disbelief, he saw the base of the City hovering above, and the length of it was twelve thousand stadia, which is one thousand, three hundred and eighty miles, and the breadth of its catching away did block out the Sun.

The rapture of the Lord, His City and His Hosts did Satan see firsthand, witnessing God removing Himself from Adam, Eve and the dire consequence of the outcome of exercising the free will He had given them. For He could in no wise be in the direct presence of their sin.

To the first heaven (where the birds fly) did the City retreat to its zenith, reaching the firmament. There did the Angels of the Four Winds open the windows of the sky and command Leviathan to withhold the Deep, protecting the east and northern windows, and another great dragon, whose appearance is as a bright red comet, was commanded to protect the rafters of the west and the southmost sides of the dome.

In a twinkling of an eye did the City of God soar through the waters above the dome, vanishing into the Third Heaven (and seven more heavens there be within the Third).

The freezing of the part of the Deep, just above the circle of the Earth, made a noise that cannot be described by the bards, neither sung by the minstrels. As the simultaneous screaming of so many jackals and the raking of innumerable fingernails upon granite was the sound. The intensity thereof caused the Adversary to cover his ears and shut his eyes, hoping self-imposed blindness would cause the sound to end.

Moments later, silence.

His eyes opened.

The Sun had returned. The cosmic freeze above had ceased. God's throne was now above the circle of the Earth, which had become solid as a sea of glass. The Creator had, formally and with a silent ascension (followed by an apocalyptic coldness from the heaven above), separated Himself from the very center of His creation. No longer did He dwell amongst Man.

And lo, while Satan looked above did thorns in an instant spring, the newly cursed Earth goading him above the ankle of his cloven hoof, thistles scratching round the knee, unwanted weeds at once above and around the thigh of his bovine limbs.

"Ah. Death... Death is not just the cessation of breathing; rather it is separation." He reasoned out the Lord's pronouncement, concluding that God, who cannot tell a lie, had dealt in truth when and where He had said *"in the day you eat thereof, surely you will die"*.

And from that moment forward did Man, separate from God, begin to die both by spirit and flesh, continuing himself through the begetting of children who in turn also would die. The mountains groaned, and the valleys wept, and the whole of the earth, from the cockroach to the elephant, looked with longing and tearful hope to the coming of a savior. The Savior who could end the sting of death.

And Satan was afraid, burdened under the weighty doom of God's prophecy concerning the cosmic conflict between the two seeds.

Whilst the Enemy of Both God and Man was slithering about, journeying in vain towards the City that was now not, the Lord had made provision, by slaying animals, to cover the naked rebellion of His children. And following this did He by the hand of angels fashion *the Sword of Power*, by which Adam (and his progeny thereafter) would gain no entry into the Garden which is in Eden.

And Adam knew his wife, Eve, and begat Cain, the firstborn mortal, made in the image of his flawed and fallen father.

The scribes and poets and bards well record the deeds of the male descendants from the dawn of time; for who doth not know how that Cain slew Abel? And of the righteousness of Seth unto Enoch?

But these men did not lie with the air, neither bring forth children by magick.

No. Mothers were required.

The histories are long on the deeds of men, and light where recording the adventures and accomplishments of women is concerned. Adam and Eve begat daughters as well. Heroines and villainesses in their own right, these silent damsels are just as important as their male counterparts, of the equal measure in value, and worthy of memorialization.

For did God the Father Himself not declare that the Devil would be crushed by the seed of a woman?! And did not God, when He cursed Woman, not also provide her with comprehension and a unique connection to salvation that even the most well-meaning gentleman will never quite know, books and psalms and poetic discourse falling short in the shadow of experience?

For childbirth doth magnify salvation!

By water and then by blood is the babe brought forth, by grievous and joyous pain into a world of grandeur and beauty and grace. The same world vile and dreadful, bound in sin and corruption. In vanishing agony, woman beholds her child, and in that moment knows what salvation is… For though the babe will disobey, will rebel, will backbite, will without ceasing bring days of worry, for him will she do anything to stand in the gap, and give all for his sanctity, growth and triumph.

For *motherhood* doth magnify salvation!

Within the curse of childbearing is contained the greatest gift, a divine understanding of how much Man pains his Creator… and how God looks upon Man, whom He loves with an immeasurable love akin to a *mother's love*.

Adam knew Eve, and Eve gave birth to Cain. And Eve did in that very moment indeed understand salvation.

Three minutes after, she understood it yet again. For delivered unto Eve was also the first lass born.

Cain, the firstborn of the Sons of Adam, was a twin, and his fair sister, whose hair was as an unkempt, swirling flame, whose cheeks were freckled ere they were ever kissed by light of the Sun, whose eyes were large round emeralds threefold more alert than the dull brutish glance of her older brother, did introduce herself to the world not with screaming and crying nor the gasp of entry that most babes give. Rather did Luluwa come with such laughter and verve that the animals gleefully considered: *'So extraordinary is Luluwa, so happy and good, that she did by reason of her joyfulness almost reverse the recent Fall of Mankind.'*

Luluwa grew to become a young woman, celebrated and adored by her parents and siblings, the whole of the blossoming earth treasuring its first princess.

But treasures draw the eyes of villains as well…

***

"Do as I direct thee, Azazel, for there is a hedge of protection around Eve, and I cannot discover how to slay her, neither harm even one hair upon her brow."

"I can no more lie with a mortal daughter of Eve than can a cow mate with a badger. Such a thing cannot be conceived in the mind of angels, or of men—"

"But of the imaginations of *devils*, there is no limit. For me, *anything* can be!" Lucifer had mastered an assumed, pretended authority that imitated the Most High. He did not need to smite or scourge the Watcher Angel before him; rather he summonsed a dark cloud bordered with dark green light that was as a tempest of judgement, a storm of dread fear.

Azazel, who was regarded as a Mighty One, was the overseer of shepherds, the one assigned to teach men how to farm and bring forth strong, healthy yield from the soils, and to ensure optimal and healthy reproduction amongst the cattle and sheep. He was winged, the height of three tall men, with his face resembling the form and fashion of his goats.

But he was as an ant before Lucifer, a cowering and shivering wet rabbit beneath the judgmental glare of an elephant.

"Do. As. Directed." The Devil had no need for feigned words of persuasion, neither made grand arguments of the philosophical justification for plotting a grave sin against creation itself. Rather, by reason of his authority did the Adversary compel the high-ranking Watcher to descend from the Third Heaven to the realm of men.

The Hosts of Heaven are corporeal beings, not spirits. They were created in a unique likeness, as the animals upon the Earth and the fowls in the air, with their own functions and according to God's purposes and creativity. Their interactions down in the world of men are a matter of geographic travel and traverse into a realm where light and the particles move at a different speed and with a different composition than found in the Third Heaven.

In this regard, heaven is a place, not a dimension. And should Man have the right type of body, his never-dying soul could surely visit the Third Heaven. But Man's soul sins, and his body goes down, not up.

But the angels can ascend and descend the ladder betwixt the two worlds, having bodies after a different sort and glory than the Sons of Adam. They are able to slow down the unseen matter that moves and flows through them, resuming either in their given form, in the form of the animals that they oversee, or in the likeness of men.

Designed to be ministering spirits unto men, signs for seasons, for planting, living declarations of the Savior to come, and hallmarks of the glory, greatness, terror and grandeur of the Lord that made them, many of the Hosts of Heaven instead deviated from their purpose, resulting in chaos, destruction and calamity throughout the cosmos.

And the first of these to leave his estates in heaven was the Goat God, Azazel.

Luluwa was to be given in marriage to her brother Abel (and Cain likewise to Abel's twin sister, that they might start in earnest to populate the world) and was yet a virgin when Azazel committed history's first rape: the Horned God violating the Virgin Princess.

At the first he loathed the act, having neither attraction nor lustful desire towards her. But doing his duty to undo and unseat God gave Azazel a pleasure, a thirst and a lustful hunger that would set the course of his occupation for the next several centuries. Such was his desire towards women – how to paint their faces, how to adorn them in alluring dress, what to cover, what to reveal, what to conceal, what jewels should adorn necks, paired with the color of the enamel upon their fingernails and toenails, and how to fix and braid their hair – that he spent every minute of every day wholly dedicated to the subject and topic of seduction and the sorcery thereof.

His thirst for women was unquenchable, consuming him with such burning lust that Lucifer had to bind him for a time in a secret cave, for he was of no fit use to any angel of God by reason of the insanity wrought by his addiction to the unnatural use of women.

And the first victim, Luluwa, in shame, in fear, and in innocence, did that which the victims of such deeds always do. She concealed the matter from Abel.

Abel was a just, kind, caring and friendly lad. Luluwa surmised that the burden of knowing his wife had been raped by a god would surely crush him and, worse, send him to a sure death in futile effort to avenge his partner. She refused to let a goat rob her of a healthy marriage and, full of wisdom and grace, bore her scars as do most women – privately.

Luluwa conceived.

Abel, of course, believing that the child was his, was overjoyous, the proudest of fathers to be. But Abel was not the father. And Luluwa, for the sum of the nine months she carried the babe, knew this by reason of the intuition and wisdom given by God to mothers.

Abel was a good man. Luluwa was a great woman. But the thing which grew inside her was neither good, nor great.

Born three hours after midnight under the incessant crying of three owls who refused to leave the rafters in the humble home where dwelt the *First Family* (for although Man had not yet mastered masonry or carpentry, Adam, who from the first possessed the intelligence to name and classify each of the animals created for domestication, had been given the basic acumen for structuring a house. Never living in caves or as the monkeys except when tyranny and poverty intentionally caused such a plight, men have ever been building-dwellers from the beginning), in equal portion and exact opposite measure did this baby announce her entry. Where Luluwa had given thankful and laughing announcement of her coming onto the stage of life did this child scream in vengeance, avarice and hate. With screeching owls, terrific pain and buckets of blood came forth the child.

Luluwa: red curls and sunshine. This child: hair straight as a razor's edge, black as tar, visage pale as new snow.

Luluwa: inviting, warm, approachable. This child: as a scorpion, adder and cactus merged into beautiful but untouchable vileness of danger and foreboding.

Luluwa: striking, comely green eyes. And this child, whom her mother and the man who thought he was her father chose to call Lilith: large crimson eyes.

And thus was Lilith, the First Nephilim, the most Elder Fae, and the Primal Witch born.

Chapter 4
The Girl with Cloven Hooves

From her birth didst Lilith have the cleft hooves like unto her father, the Watcher Azazel. With much cunning speed, swaddling and maximizing advantage of Abel's modest reverence for his wife's privacy, Luluwa could conceal *this* aberration.

But by the eighth day did a development unfurl that could not be hidden by clothing, neither concealed by tricks with hair or the manipulation of candlelight and shadows.

Sprouting from the sides and shoulder blades of Lilith…
Wings.

Lilith was a red-eyed owl from the beginning. A night demon whose very existence cried 'Abomination!' to the creatures around her and to the God above who made them all. She judged them and their deeds done at night that she alone could see with hypocrisy and envy.

For God did create life to reproduce after its own kind. Lilith was outside of the creation, yet not a new thing: rather a bastardized composite of two classes of beings. Two creatures made for good, when combined, produce that which is bad. For the best of oil and vinegar do not mix, lest they give way to black tar.

The untoward intent to foil God's plans for His creation was so focused and aimed with such vicious intent by the madness of the rebel that sired her that Lilith was a villainess from birth, forged only for the singular and evil purpose of thwarting God's prophecy.

A goddess. The supreme of her kind.

Luluwa, who is the forebearer of all healthy marriages, did quickly shelve her own shame upon the altar of honesty, confessing to Abel that she had not been a virgin when they wedded, and that one of the Elect Angels above had cruelly abused her.

Abel straightway removed himself from her presence, but not out of malice towards his love; rather that his weeping and bloodlust might not frighten or further discourage her. Towards the Garden which is in Eden, to the place where the City of God once was, did he hasten, knowing not elsewhere to cry out to the Father.

Adam joined the distressed lad, and Cain, his brother, too sought where they might beseech the Lord.

Eve remained with her daughter and granddaughter, feeding and – where they could negotiate about her wings – snuggling and cuddling the spawn of sin. For the pot can in no wise be charged with the crimes of the potter, neither did it ask to be sculpted in the first place.

To the entrance of the Garden of Eden did the three men advance – and no further, for the Cherub with his blade of flame they could not breach.

But God is no respecter of 'place' or formality; He is the God of Relationships. Hearing them holler from right where they stood, rendering their journey good for the sake of bodily exercise and vain for all else, God met Man where Man was, and not the reverse. *For what man can approach a holy God?*

The glory of the Lord appeared first, and the overwhelming light thereof did prostrate the men, an unseen force flattening their palms and faces upon the cool grass. Instantly they were filled with fear. A fear wrought of awe; a reverence housed in glory.

Adam, who had afore walked with the Lord in the cool of the day, no less overcome with the power and greatness of Lord, was at the same time smiling in the dirt, seeing the ashen visages of his sons. For this fear brings joy and wonder, not dread, knocking mortal men to the ground for the wonder and warmth of it, and not for groveling and shamefacedness.

Bidding the men rise, the Son of God spoke with the three men. He appeared before them as a man of three decades: bearded, handsome, and fierce. But also amicable, parental, and regal.

God enquired of each man how that he might adjudicate the matter with Azazel.

Cain spoke first. Having a quick mouth fueled by a hot head operated by a slow brain, he required vengeance upon the angel, beseeching the Lord with much imprecation to let Abel crush the fiend's skull upon the rocks with many large stones.

Then Abel, who suffered greatly in his mind, seeing again and again what he perceived in his imagination had befallen his bride, gave the more prudent answer, saying, "Lord God, I know not how to answer the matter until my own wrath, which is like unto the hypocrite, is assuaged." Through gritted teeth, the humble lad continued, "For how can one flawed creature judge another, especially when filled with naught else but wrath? Forgive me first, O God, and when in right standing before you, only then show me the answer. Not my will, neither my own understanding, but on you only will I lean. For you are the rock of my salvation."

God so favored the faith and wisdom of Abel that, for a moment, He appeared to have forgotten that Adam, too, was part of the spontaneously convened council. During the discourse with Abel, while God soothed and promised him that all would ultimately work in accord with His plan for the Ages and reminded the boy to never lose hope or joy, the Lord did not so much as look at Adam.

Then after a long pause did God, who is the author and inventor of timing and humor, look to Adam, chuckling with such might that it shook the earth and caused nearby trees to shed their leaves, and saying, "I'm sorry, Adam. Anything to add?"

Adam, who had experienced nearly one hundred and fifty years of life, loved all his children equally, differently, and deeply. Having a concerned but understanding disposition towards Cain and a bursting pride and admiration for Abel, whose wisdom already matched or surpassed his own, the proud father could only contribute: "Would that you heal Abel's heart and then visit upon the Watcher that way of justice proposed by Cain. But let no blood be shed by the hand of Man, O Lord, lest it give him a thirst of it."

God blessed the words and wisdom of Abel, and worried after Cain, whom He also loved. Wanting to share more but knowing that his children, here at the dawn of creation, could not receive it, He reasserted the instruction: "Be fruitful and multiply, have dominion over the earth, and in kindness and strength be ye just stewards thereof." Following this, He gave continued reassurance that Azazel would be dealt with in his time.

Adam trusted.

Abel trusted but suffered.

Cain was bitter, wanting the justice that was right in his eyes *straight away*.

* * *

Obeying the Lord, Abel and Luluwa reared Lilith as they could and continued to make babies: glorious, wholesome, cheerful children – an abundance of blessing for hearth and home.

Lilith hated her siblings and would have wrung them by the neck or hurled them from the high cliff, but her angelic father made her delay the act. Azazel had returned to his estate above the firmament (the Watchers at this time still had residency and access in the heavenly realms), but was able to communicate to her through dreams, in visions, and through the development of Occult Sciences.

He did not discourage her malice nor her insatiable desire to slay the younger children (who now numbered five sisters and six brothers), only because her full purpose, to be revealed when she had come to womanhood, might be foiled through the calamity that would surely ensue among the elders should she commit murder so young.

In the process of time, Lilith attained her fourteenth year, and was activated.

Her first charge: **corrupt the seed of Adam**. Most directly.

Her grandfather she would endeavor to seduce, and get children by the object of the Creator's first prophecy.

Lilith, the winged fowl, had grown beautiful in her own way. In form she was mostly as a young woman: slender, curvy, tall and pale. That her eyes were wholly red, that her lower legs from the calf down were like unto a goat, that she had two full sets of wings (one at the top of her shoulders, another beginning just above her hip bones), and that her teeth were lichen-like did not diminish her attraction. In fact, for many men, her animalistic (for many of the Hosts of Heaven were created to help Man oversee and steward animals, and thus do the animals look like their divine rulers) attributes were forbidden, attractive, and seductive.

But Adam, who had already hurled the world towards a destiny with judgement and death, was not to be taken by a *forbidden fruit* a second time. Adam had one wife: his goddess, Eve, who is the Mother of all the Living.

The sin of the one by whom death came had produced a repentant, wise man who walked closely with the Lord and guarded well his passions, bringing them under subjection.

Lilith did first directly attempt to lie with him, finding occasion when he was working the field. Kind but firm, he instructed her to turn her desires to whom Abel might select for her. Moreover, Adam showed Lilith much grace, knowing that she was not like unto the daughters of Men, and perhaps unable to control herself in this regard.

A second time she threw herself at the First Man, and again he turned her away.

And a third.

Only on this occasion, Adam could not conceal the wanton behavior from Eve (for heretofore he had sheltered the dignity of the lass and contained the matter), who came upon Lilith aggressively groping at Adam's member, doing all to reveal his nakedness in the openness of the day.

"Banish her!" Eve commanded Luluwa, the ferocity of jealousy boiling behind Mother Eve's eyes.

"She is a child – she is my child!" responded the First Daughter, pleading with her mother, beseeching her for mercy.

"Your child is a child of a devil, and would undo us all." Eve's words were cold. And coldly delivered. To kill or administer capital punishment did not exist within the heart of Man at this time, only to remove the malefactor from being able to actively continue his or her untoward deeds. "Your daughter is a bird, Luluwa. Get her from our gardens and our men, and like unto the birds kept as pets for the children, cage her."

Luluwa would not enjoy victory, neither convince Eve to usher a lesser sentence, for the hand of Lilith had been but five minutes removed from her husband's loins and jealousy is the rage of men, *and women*. Thus, Luluwa could negotiate in degrees of severity only, seeing no path for acquittal.

"There is a cave two days' journey from here. I am fond of it and can fashion it as a dwelling for Lilith, banishing her from amongst us. May I see to this in the stead of a cage?" she pleaded.

Although Eve responded to Luluwa, her stare was fixed on Adam. "Instruct the smith to forge a cage, placing it in the cave where Lilith will make her home. Let the cage gaze upon her, threaten her, stalk her as a daily reminder that the bird has one chance to behave itself, or her living tomb it will become."

Chapter 5
The First Murder

In the world that was before the Great Flood, there was no rain, neither inclement weather. Subterranean caverns filled with waters sourced from rivers, rivers from the ocean, and the ocean from the Deep.

God formed the mountains by design to be at once beautiful and asymmetrical: awe and art, crafted in grooves and crags. As a king heats the wax, pressing the seal of his signet ring with forceful purpose and delicate design upon the vellum, in this manner did the Lord form the earth, the canvas He wrought by the Word of power.

In the beginning, in the world that was, all the land was gathered in the center of one continuous middle earth. And caves have always been, for water seeks its level, and in an instant fills and shapes arteries that run from the highest peaks to the lowest depths of the sea.

True to Eve's sentence, Luluwa confined the young lass Lilith to a life of house arrest within the frightening and beautiful marvel of one of God's primal hollows.

Cave-life is not solitude, respite, and bliss. Cave-life is darkness, fear, and pitch-black madness. Sound confuses, and flickers of firelight beguile with false shapes and distorted sizes.

A faint whisper in a hollow hill vibrates as a great drum, the sound bouncing and deflecting throughout the caverns, creating great confusion as to its direction, source, and origin. Every click is disorienting, every clap causing unbalance. How much more the thunderous the wings of haughty and dread Azazel!

The shadow of a mouse appears as a bear, and by proportion an actual bear casts no shadow at all, rather filling the whole of the natural hall, only the glimmer of his eyes announcing his unwelcome intrusion. How much more the height and girth of the great goat god Azazel!

The fallen angel had ceased communicating by arcane means, opting for a face-to-face approach. He made rough and contested descent down through the firmament, defeating the faithful angels who fought bravely, yet in vain, to detain him.

For those who are evil expend great energy simply to berate or belittle those under their authority. For this purpose did he hasten unto his daughter.

"You are a failure." There was neither effort of speech, nor posturing with poetry; no forethought of tone and punctuation. Rather cold, cruel, brief words.

But the Screech Owl was resilient. "And what causes you to believe that my success or failure is measured by what you think, Father?"

"I could kill you with no more effort than the elephant crushes the ant, having no awareness that it has spoiled his home, or slain a score of his kinsman." Being upon the earth again, in the realm of men *and women,* kindled Azazel's lust, causing immediate and all-consuming thoughts of what he had done to Luluwa. "And simply try again to make another one like you."

"I do not think that you could or would lightly slay me, for where would my soul go? I am outside the view of God's creation. Your analogy fails."

"How so?" Azazel puffed, indignant.

"I am not an ant."

"No?"

"Nay. I am a caterpillar. And none know what might emerge, should you release me from this cocoon of flesh!"

Lilith's response was brilliant, and accurate. Azazel, bereft of response, did naught but glare. She in kind, with crimson eyes a lambent looking-glass by the light of the humble firepit that warmed her prison-home, glared up at the winged goat. And no fear was found in her.

But a third party had crept in unseen, a witness to the confrontation. He made no sound, watching in perfect silence, enjoying the malice for maliciousness's sake.

Satan wanted to say something brooding and brilliant. He desired to puff his own grandeur, uttering words of great authority that demonstrated his power and glory above the other naughty angels formerly in God's employ.

Alas, he could not. For at this, his first witness of Lilith in her defiant magnificence – the best aspects of the daughters of Eve and the heavenly beings combined in her singularly unique form – was Satan enamored and amorous towards the girl.

"You are not a failure, my little white owl."

The extra participant startled Lilith, who clenched fists and turned towards the Devil, in appearance as a handsome man, shrouded in the light of the mouth of the cave.

Gliding towards her, he gently gathered both fists into his hand, then eased them, changing them from a ball at once back into ten thin and comely fingers. Returning control of her hands to their owner, he caressed her cheek with the back of one hand whilst adjusting the rebellious feathers of her raven-like hair, so that her face could be recovered from dishevelment.

"Adam is a faithful man, honoring Eve, though the heavens fall and the whole of humanity suffers death because of her." Towards Lilith was he hot, to Azazel cold. "It was a bad plan."

"There is no better way to soil the water than poisoning the fount," Azazel argued.

"The fount is faithful to its wife. We must kill the droplets as they form and fall. As your sweet daughter has always dreamed, yes?"

"My brothers and sisters live in great lodges, and the young men continue to learn and invent new comforts and structures by the day. They are in wealth and plenty. I in the high crag of a mountain, marked and exiled under threat of living in *that!*" Lilith pointed to a great cage forged of iron core, glazed and folded with alloy, bronze and copper by one of Adam's sons, the Smith, who labored under the tutelage and instruction of an angel of God. "I am in a prison dwelling next to threat of a double-prison!" the Screech Owl raged. "From the moment they were born have I hated the children of Luluwa and Abel, and by extension, the house of Adam and Eve. And daily doth the hatred kindle."

"You thirst for blood?"

"I thirst," she responded. And the tone of her simple reply gave even the Prince of Darkness pause, such is the authority of hate and hurt and malice.

"Then drink, little white owl. Hunt and drink."

The Devil did plot with Lilith, the fifteen-year-old she-devil, that she would leave the place of her imprisonment under the cover of night – of that very night, testing for the first time her ability to make aerial use of her appendages and exercising her night vision in earnest, for to snatch an infant from its bed and return to the cave, there to kill him.

There was neither guard nor seneschal at this time, for Man did not yet know war, neither had violence entered the heart of Man. The Screech Owl was at once upon the ledge of a great, arched opening in the side of a wooden home: a window before the time of glassworks, where only ornate curtains adorned with stitchwork and dyed zoomorphic and knotwork forms separated the home from the gentle winds and the breezy mists. Her feet, being as a goat, did not allow the owl to perch, but the effect was similar; the rapidity of her wings gave her the appearance of a floating, or perched, menace.

The dwelling was storied. Cows and goats stabled below, and the family in various simple room apartments above.

A son of Luluwa, not yet four, slept with a persistent smile next to his older sister. She had rolled away from the lad in the depth of her slumber, leaving not so much as an arm snugly draped over him to guard from the monsters that haunt children in the night.

For there were no monsters in the night… not before Azazel got Lilith by Luluwa.

But now did history's first night terror unfold, and 'twas no dream nor vision brought by fever. For effortlessly did Lilith snatch the boy, who could neither scream nor protest, but only look upon the face of beautiful evil as he ascended in her arms to the apex of the first heaven.

True terror caused his face to become ashen. White as a ghost. White as Lilith, whom he beheld.

The terror of heights, for what man's feet had ever left the safe and comforting soil? Man was intended to walk, not to fly.

The terror of helplessness. His little body reactively shut down, becoming calm, becoming still. He didn't flail, squirm, or strike out at his rapidly ascending captor.

The terror of her face. Lilith had a visage like unto Eve: beautiful, authoritative, and perfect. But the comparisons failed at the teeth, as Eve, the Mother of all the Living, was not a fanged, cursed thing. Lilith's frontmost four teeth, both upper and lower sets, were as unto the mortals, only far brighter and whiter in glory. But beginning at the fifth, and thence all the way to the back into her cheeks and jawline, did Lilith have rows of fangs which were as the teeth of a shark, only perfect, small, and proportionate to the shape of her mouth. And frontmost were the two top fangs longer, prominent, speckled with blood nicked from her own lips.

Most of all, the terror of her eyes, for they were all soul and no soul. All darkness but all flame. They judged him worthy of guilt, though he was three. They judged him with death, though he knew no crime.

Petrified and helpless, he fainted. And in the sleep of faint formed, by his famous little habit, a smile.

Lilith held him as one holds their lover in a pool, the water producing weightless scooping at the knees and about the shoulders. By a nature unknown to the caged bird, her cradle was gentle. And during the flight to place of execution did the Screech Owl suffer defeat: not from a towering goat god with bulging muscles atop bulging muscles crowned by more bulging muscles, nor by his master, the Master bathed in lying lights, ever singing deceptive songs. Nay: 'twas the natural affection given by God to all women.

The first murder was arrested.

Chapter 6
The Consort of Satan

"I could not do it."

The Primal Witch, though yet a damsel, spoke with the authority of a long-reigning sovereign. She saluted Satan as neither lord nor master.

"But, my owl, you did proclaim such hot hatred for them. I will help you. I know not that an angel can slay one of these apes" – for, as yet, no person had suffered death by any reason, not by malice nor illness or calamity nor any cause – "or whether He Himself," the Prince of Darkness cast a mocking glance upwards towards the Father of Lights, "will appear and stay my hand, peradventure to scourge me for the deed." The Devil was this day full of overmuch bravery as a schoolboy is in the company of the lass he dotes upon, for Lucifer did long ever to be in the company of Lilith.

But it was not reciprocated. Her coldness and plainness of speech persisted.

"He is not here," she said. "I returned him to his sibling's side, hoping that he wakes only to fret about a dream or frightening vision."

"Why do you rebel against me?" the Devil demanded, bedazzlement giving way to anger.

"Why did you rebel against *Him*?" she countered. And this time admired her work, allowing a slight smirk to form.

"I have no temperament for philosophy, damsel."

The cave was very cold inside, yet the humidity just outside the mouth of the dwelling produced an odd combination whereby the occupants were simultaneously sweating and shivering. Lucifer, in his manifestation and form of man, did sweat as a man, and wiped his brow whilst his lips, blue from the cold, did press together in scolding pose. Clenching one fist, he approached.

"Will you then strike *your white owl*?" Having no fear, Lilith stood tall, bracing for what might come.

Though he did in earnest desire to humble the lass with his fist, the Devil did pause, noting her words, and marvel at her unwavering bravery. Instead, he questioned her. "We must prevent the seed of the Woman from coming forth, by all devices. And culling them ere they bring forth more of their kind must need be paramount in our enterprise. Why could you not take vengeance on those who did shame and exile thee?"

"Eve is accountable for her actions, and I shall deal with Eve." Lilith gazed away, thinking upon the infant she had but recently cradled in flight. "But the lad did naught to harm me. Let every person be accountable for their own actions."

Lucifer ignored the logic, but noted the gaze. "You were fond of him. And your mercy may be our destruction," he judged.

Here did the Devil bid Lilith resume her life of solitude in the cave, threatening to return with further instruction after exploring the matter himself. Should he (or Azazel), as a being from heaven, be permitted to kill a man, her employ would have no use to him. But if some divine decree and the force of the Hosts of Heaven suffered him not to harm the seed of Adam and Eve, the Prince of Darkness would again call upon his owl for further plotting and malevolence.

As the Fallen One made his departure, he looked once more upon the immovable witch. In the line of his gaze he noted the special cage wrought for her. And he noted well how much she loathed it.

***

"*[3] And in process of time it came to pass that Cain brought of the fruit of the ground an offering unto the Lord.*

[4] And Abel, he also brought of the firstlings of his flock and of the fat thereof. And the Lord had respect unto Abel and to his offering:

⁵ *But unto Cain and to his offering he had not respect. And Cain was very wroth, and his countenance fell.*

⁶ *And the Lord said unto Cain, Why art thou wroth? and why is thy countenance fallen?*

⁷ *If thou doest well, shalt thou not be accepted? and if thou doest not well, sin lieth at the door. And unto thee shall be his desire, and thou shalt rule over him.*

⁸ *And Cain talked with Abel his brother: and it came to pass, when they were in the field, that Cain rose up against Abel his brother, and slew him."*

***

Satan had rightly surmised that he could not directly harm a man, or a woman. For when he would attack Eve, Michael, the Captain of Angels himself, and Gabriel, his great and faithful ally, would appear, and drive the serpent from the scene.

Many years passed between the time that Lilith caused history's first nightmare and the dread afternoon when, by *beguilement* and the ongoing discovery and mastery of the flawed and failing nature of Man, did Satan – who was sin lying in wait at the door of opportunity – nudge Cain in the direction of doom, gleefully looking on as he by jealousy and envy did kill faithful Abel.

By Adam did sin enter, and death by sin, and the first death (not the separation with God, which was instant in the Garden, but rather of the physical sort) by murder at the hand of Adam's son, Cain.

Man had multiplied greatly upon the earth, and early cities and settlements had appeared in but a few generations. There was much work to do, and the dark heart of the Devil returned in thought to the Screech Owl, considering that perhaps something had changed in the order and outworking of things. If God would not let him directly shed blood, maybe now that blood had been shed by the failings of men themselves, He might permit the world's first abomination to shed more. The nature of reality, the lighting and ebb and flow of Paradise, seemed a shade darker. Satan delighted in this and made haste for the cave.

Prior to the Fall, Lucifer had many complimentary names and titles, one of which was the Anointed Cherub. For originally, he was a Cherub, a class of heavenly being having:
- The face of a man;
- The face of an ox;
- The face of an eagle;
- The face of a lion.

Each of these features was designed by the Lord from the foundation of the world to glorify some aspect of His Son, who would become a man and the Savior of all men.
- The face of the man glorified the Messiah's humanity;
- The face of the ox, the Messiah's work as a servant;
- The face of the eagle, the Messiah's royalty;
- The face of the lion, the Messiah's divinity.

For all the Hosts of Heaven by nature, construct and purpose point to the Son of God, the constellations themselves telling His story every night, the stars declaring Him.

Each of the Cherubim were alike in features, but Lucifer was special. His body was a garment of every precious jewel, his glory did shine above the noonday sun, and musical instruments did adorn the ethereal body that encased such a comely spirit. The grandness of his wingspan, the flapping of which caused birds to chirp and flowers to bloom, did cover the throne of God. Lucifer would often hover above the throne, creating an actual canopy of winged, jeweled glory.

In this manifestation did he appear unto Lilith, strolling up to her, one remarkable and hooved being to another.

"My little white owl, you age not, save to come into the fullness of womanhood, and your beauty hath surpassed Luluwa, your mother, and Eve, the Mother of all the Living."

Lilith was not yet mad over her prison, but she had given herself to bitterness, and did not suffer fools – even gloriously appearing angelic fools. "I will not kill the innocent," she started. "They—"

"There are none good, for all sin, and one day all will die, Lilith." The conversation interrupted by decades resumed without so much as a parenthesis. Only now, Satan felt like engaging in philosophy. "I am only asking you to help me prevent the coming of the Promised Seed by expediting that reality."

"I cannot kill children," she told him, resolute.

"Dearest. Something has changed. A man has been slain!" The Shining One reveled in the thought. "Tangible, actual death is amongst men, and shall reign. I shall be its king, and you my consort."

Suddenly, another being from the above realm joined the reunion.

"See there now, your father the Great Shephard Azazel has come too, that we might reason together."

Azazel was brutish, but pleading and articulate. "Hunt young male offspring. Thin their numbers that peradventure we may eliminate the seed of the Woman, or reduce the potential for His coming. Moreover, get thee back into the grace of Eve that you may abort the prophecy at its source."

"Why cannot YOU do these things?" she shrieked at both of them.

"He does not permit us. It appears that we need a monster for the task." Lucifer, in the twinkling of an eye, was again as a man. "A beautiful, fanged, seductively pale, and winged monster."

"If you are still bound by His permission, then you are still under the authority of the Most High, and no God." Lilith sought the area of Satan's greatest weakness, *pride*, and pierced it without mercy. "Plotting and scheming to thwart the prophecy of God, and you yet do not comprehend that you are but an agent for His own purpose and plan for the Ages? I can do more like unto the Creator than thou, for I am a woman and can bring forth life, and you cannot. And it seems that I can by my hand, like Him, take life, and you cannot. What are you but a ministering spirit, Lord Lucifer?"

"When I am finished with you, wife, you will be no woman and all monster, and for your defiance, a ministering spirit you will be unto me. For I will be your God and you my avenging angel."

"I will not kill innocent children." Lilith stated the facts again. "Neither can I gain the grace of Eve, for her jealousy burns hot forever, and we are at irreconcilable ends." More facts.

"You will be forever known as a menace upon the earth. An abomination of desolation. A killer of babes. The ruin of blissful rest. And when your infamous, murderous ways are published to the four corners of the Earth, then will Eve, exhausted and weary by the knowledge of your deeds, seek thee out for to make a treaty. And then you, Lilith, will use the occasion to murder she who is to issue the Seed."

Lucifer's declaration was as official as a hot brand upon the ass of a steed. He would not be deterred. He would both at once punish Lilith and make her his bride.

***

Lucifer raped Lilith whilst in the likeness of a man, and after the passing of nine moons, a child did she bear unto the Devil.

***

She could not overcome the fallen Watchers, the Titans of Old who, along with mortal agents given to corruption, restrained, guarded and greatly multiplied the restrictions of the already imprisoned goddess. A natural prison in the form of a cave and a mother's loving edict had become an actual prison complete with keepers on a rotating shift, day and night, who controlled the lighting, the water sources, and the supply of food for Satan's unwilling bride.

When the child was delivered, Lilith was permitted to hold him for the space of one half-hour. Time ceased for her then, and the bond she formed and the love she knew was mightier than the torture of ten thousand devils. *For mothers can bear any pain, but to hold their children.*

But even for Lilith, a supernatural being and the first of her kind, the limits were found. Found in one specially devised cage.

Satan had remembered the *cage within the cage*, how that the Owl looked upon it with fearful hate, knowing that its mystical design would somehow agonize and contain her. And at last, her terror was fulfilled, for he did strip her of the babe violently and lock her in the oversized birdcage.

The door latched. The lock clicked. She changed forever.

Above even the violation of her body did the imprisonment of the winged demi-deity press as an anvil upon her soul. To Lilith, freedom was the highest good. When banished to a cave, it suffered and she suffered; when locked in a cage, liberty's flame flickered. Her choice was either to resolve to survive the imprisonment, hoping to one day again fan the flicker into a blaze, or succumb to her chains and yield to a sentence of eternal slavery.

She chose the former, bracing for what might be next in her life of doom. Vigilant for opportunity at escape.

What was next reached new depths of intentional evil.

A man, a slave of sorts, presented, within an outstretched arm's reach, another baby. A second man held the newborn son of Lilith and Lucifer.

"Are you now ready to hunt the Sons of Adam, or would you see your own perish?" Satan asked.

Here did he diabolically put Lilith in a vice, seeking to trap her by her own reasoning. She would not kill the son of Abel because of Eve's transgressions, for the individual child was innocent. How now could she choose to kill her own child, also innocent, though he be a monster?

"One must die?" she asked, her knuckles white, clenching the bars.

"One must die," Satan confirmed.

Lilith refused to engage the Devil eye to eye, rather looking directly into the eyes of her son, saying goodbye.

"Would that none perish, but better the one half of you that is your father perish, that the whole of humanity might continue and be saved."

"Then you do it," raged the angry fallen angel – the false god of men and inventor of all religion, the ruler of the world who could not control one winged girl. "For if I do it, his suffering will be part of every sad sonnet forevermore."

"You would harm your son to punish your wife?" Now she looked at him. A sharp and judgmental look.

"I would that my wife did as I bade her. As Eve doth for Adam, and Luluwa your mother did for Abel."

"Adam and Abel are gentle men. No woman will bow unto tyranny, neither in this world or the world to come. If men are decreed to lead, then let men be good leaders. Moreover," the sharp look was now sharper still, "submission in a relationship is based upon love, not power and advantage."

The men in league with Satan marveled at the words of Lilith.

"Do you love me?" Satan transformed back into the shining shimmer of his splendor.

"I love you not," said Lilith, wringing the neck of their son, and killing a portion of her soul in so doing.

She slumped down in her cage. Its circumference was equal to her height, so she could sit or manage to uncomfortably lie down within the structure. She collapsed in a sitting pose, her head upon her knees, her wings covering her as a shield or tent.

The lifeless body of her abomination was removed from the dwelling, and Satan gave his mortal ministers (each of whom was a son of Cain) instructions to learn the impact of torturing and then murdering the other child as well. That her choice was vain and that both children would die greatly satisfied Satan. But he would store that painful truth as a weapon with which to poke his spouse on another day.

She was not a monster. Not yet. Satan was patient, and had work to do.

Thus did he repeat the violation, causing her to conceive again. Nine months hence did she both hold and bid farewell to another child.

And nine months hence, another.

For the fourth pregnancy, Satan forced one of his priests to go in unto her, wondering if her position might change with a mortal father, inverting the offspring from one-fourth man and three-fourths devil to almost all Son of Adam.

But the outcome differed not. Each time, Lilith sacrificed her own child that the children of Adam and Eve might live.

Chapter 7
The Bird Has Flown the Coop

Women know things. And amongst women, mothers know most.

Luluwa knew by her own insight that malfeasance had befallen her daughter, and that the abomination that had made her abomination was responsible. She could intuit that Lilith was under duress, yet somehow yet alive.

Luluwa was not idle, even as months gave way to years. There were scores of rescue attempts. But as soon as she neared the base of the mount where Lilith dwelt in her cage, the very originator of the calamity that scourged Luluwa and Abel, that hedonistic goat Azazel, would arrest her efforts.

Such was Azazel's lust towards Luluwa that Lucifer did order angels to guard over him, not wanting to incur the open wrath of the Almighty for again abusing His elect lady. For Satan is cunning, and seeing his head not yet bruised by year one hundred, neither by two hundred and three score years from the beginning of all things, did he determine that God's plans would unfold slowly: here a little and there a little. Thus did the Adversary mirror his foe, resolving likewise to play the long game.

The men in Luluwa's life were terrified of rumors surrounding primal monsters in the hills, and even the bravest of them had not yet learned war. Man did till the ground and replenish the earth, he did build and discover art and song, but violence was rare and murder rarer still, let alone the structured and strategic murder that is war.

The will of men to help was present, but persisting above this was confusion and fear. And fear begat inertia, and thus did early mankind leave Lilith to the mercy of her *husband,* to be humiliated, tortured, and worse, framed and molded over many years.

By the tenth babe, Lilith developed a short song: history's first nursery rhyme, wherein she sang melodic mumblings of threatening to slay Satan, save the children and restore the world to mothers, to fathers, and to light.

By the twentieth rape, her person shattered as a felled looking-glass. Some shards were large and dominant, others slender, and some remaining bits as sparkles and sandy dust. Where once there was one Lilith, a myriad of Liliths now governed within the labyrinthine corridors of her mind, each one competing night and day to control the host that was their increasingly dark queen.

By the forty-seventh ritual of the false choice that ever resulted in the loss of two innocents, Lilith began to giggle and mock Satan, goading him over and over again that he was no god and, where carnal relations were concerned, no man either. As she mocked she would kiss him deeply, opening the inside of his cheek with her fangs.

Angered at his wife, who grew more broken and emboldened and increasingly boisterous, he devised a new plan, which he forecast aloud after a particularly violent session with his wife.

"Is it true that owls dislike water, but especially loathe the immersion therein?"

***

Luluwa, although she could not physically overpower the Goat God, nonetheless refused to give up hope of one day discovering a path to her child. For this cause, she never chose the same path twice, very often bearing a small scythe, hacking and whacking through bush and thorn, ascending the mountain via rough, steep spots where no foot had trodden.

The work typically resulted in exhaustion and injury, even if she was discovered only a few hours into her desperate work by Azazel. Often she reckoned that she would count herself victorious just to see her firstborn once more, even if that meant dying during the enterprise, but one day as she climbed she noticed a calm quietness, and the lack of impediment of her journey.

The deer played with the red-haired first princess of men, and the rabbits ran to and fro at her feet. The mountain, being absent of devils, was rejuvenated, the earth herself making happy, healing vibrations in support of the tired feet of the favored daughter.

As Luluwa approached the mouth of the cave, happiness, fear, and nerves spiraled as an unyielding helix in her bowels. *What will I find? Am I prepared for this? Does my girl think I have abandoned her? Does she hate me?*

The bundle of nerves did not unravel her resolve, however. The Widow, the Princess, the greatest of the daughters of Eve, forced herself by her own will to run as quickly as her legs would carry her into the mouth of the dark abode.

Empty.

The fire that lit the domicile was recent; was dying but viable enough that Luluwa was able to restore its breath and light the dwelling.

Empty.

And more than empty. Empty with great effort, for even the cage within the cave was no more.

As the flame rose within the cave, so too the hope that Lilith lived rose within her mother. For the evidence demonstrated relocation and not execution. *Hasty* relocation, which explained why the rescue attempt had been uncontested.

But relocated where? Lilith was a vagabond and terror, the mythology already developing, along with whispers of her connection to lost children. That she may have been forcibly moved only to be murdered elsewhere or that myriad other maladies might have befallen her daughter seized Luluwa's hope, and strangled it.

Slowing her breathing and controlling the strange combination of sweat from the outside and shiver within the natural hall of the cave, she whispered, "They are gone; I am alone."

Falling to her knees, she cried to God the question asked more often over the course of the ages and generations of Men than are sands of the sea, and thrice the number of stars in heaven. *Why.* Why does God permit evil? Why does He allow these things to happen?

Later men, generations after Luluwa, were required to walk by faith and not by sight, yet she had an advantage that, at the dawn of time when God walked more directly with His special creation, she just might receive an answer.

A direct answer.

An *audible* answer.

The glory of the Lord manifested in the cave, filling it with light and a haze of white-hot warmth.

No man (or woman) has seen God the Father, who is a spirit, but He does manifest in the person of God the Son, who has the form of celestial flesh, and who embraced and comforted Luluwa with a hug never equaled again amongst the living, not from the foundation of the world to the dispensation of the fullness of time. This is the very embrace that the Savior of the World will give to each of His children when they have resurrected into the glory of the age to come.

Where sometimes God deploys His angels as ministering spirits, knowing what had befallen Luluwa at the hands of those created to help, not harm, the daughters of Eve, and being sensitive to her hurts, the Lord ministered unto her Himself. He gave to her in the 'now' what the remainder of His believers will only receive in the 'hereafter.'

Luluwa was history's first rape victim, first widow, and first mother of monsters. Yet never bitter; ever a victor, never a victim; a queen; a leader; a calm and nurturing wife and partner; a lover of her husband, family, and neighbors. Hers was a remarkable life.

She, along with her infinite locks of red hair, was drawn into the folds of the Lord's robes so intensely that her head disappeared and only the locks remained. The Lord noted the childlike intensity with which she did cleave unto Him, and He noted the wild hair, and the volume thereof.

The red hair did tickle His beard and bother His face. He suffered it long, but alas, let out a great laugh at the matter. And the laughter of the Lord dried every tear; the radiance of the cave became a beacon of love, cascading light above the brightness of the sun.

It pleased God to answer the question of 'Why' from the blessed Lady. He attempted to help her understand how that

He would not usurp free will or the liberty that accompanies choice but at the same time, in the restitution of all things, He would see His will done. Gently and patiently, He shared His purpose of the Ages with Luluwa, explaining how (but not when) He would restore the Earth and reconcile Himself to men. He shared the counsel and plan of the Godhead with His faithful daughter, even the details concerning the return of the Great City. The Lord withheld only His plans to reconcile the heavenly places, which was a mystery she could not understand, and that He would not reveal for another four millennia. But He had given her a more complete and colored sketch of the workings and purpose of the Great Painter than even the future prophets would receive. And He gave her the embrace of Paradise.

Then He departed. Luluwa was again alone in the cave. Filled with wisdom from on high, filled with resolve.

She was alone, and then she wasn't alone.

For in the Devil's haste to relocate the carriage of his bride to a faraway lake (the earth at this time had no continents, as all the land was one mass, but the place of the lake would later be called *Broceliande* in the enchanted forest of the Bretons), did he fail to keep Azazel under watchful chain and muzzle.

Luluwa had seen God the Son; now she looked upon a horned, cloven-hoofed angel in the self-same hour. Azazel had not known Luluwa for above six decades, and expended the pent frustration of his restrictions and punishments upon her. She did not survive the attack.

The first violation of Luluwa begat Lilith; the second violation of Luluwa begat death.

***

"Plunge me into the depth, that I might, by reason of drowning, sleep forever in the Deep."

A long metal hook was inserted within a grooved wheel, whose spokes were wooden dowels fixed to a base that allowed one man, using a crank handle, to raise or lower the cage with minimal effort. Already immersed to her neck, and loathing the soak and grunge of her wings, Lilith did hate and loathe the water and long for death. She hoped that the perpetual morose bondage of her life might finally come to an end. Her captor and husband had miscalculated, for she would but drink down death into her lungs when submerged.

But her captor was cunning. With a spear, one of his accomplices would pierce her below the lungs, causing her to involuntarily scream in agony and vomit any water consumed. Moreover, she was a supernatural being and could suffer, but perhaps not die. This was the Devil's assumption, as Lilith was the only of her kind, and none knew what might really happen to the caged bird.

Thus a new ritual began.

Forced impregnation.

False choice.

Murder of the child (children).

Drowning to the point of death.

Puncture, and resuscitation.

Satan carefully noted how each pregnancy and ritual killing affected Lilith, instructing a scribe to capture them in a book in the language of heaven.

Her pale skin became gray, losing its shine. Her hair faded from black to all white, not one strand of raven beauty remaining. Round the orbit of her red eyes formed a glowing green.

The normal processes of digestion ceased. She had no lunar issue of blood. In time she had no blood whatsoever, only sludge, a black bile circulating through her system. Yet the shell of her beauty remained.

Most days she bobbed in her cage as dead. This continued unto the hundredth baby.

"Do you love me, my little Screech Owl?" the Devil asked.

"For a century I have known nothing else save you. What might be the object of my love if not you? For there is nothing else, but perhaps my mother far away." At last, Lilith wept.

Her weeping invigorated the King of All That is False and Untrue. "Your mother perished fifty and three years ago, dearest." Her concession of power caused the happy Deceiver to offer morsels of kindness, which were only feigned in part. He did not disclose the manner of Luluwa's passing.

"Then only in this life have I you," she conceded, nearing total defeat. "Does Eve yet live?"

"The Mother of all the Living prospers, content and wealthy in her life of plenty."

"Would you still have me kill her?" she asked with sincerity which was only feigned in part.

"I would," the Prince of Darkness answered, beaming.

"And what more, that I might loose my bonds, or else sleep forever in this lake?"

"Give me one child that is not passed through the fire or wrung at the neck. Do this, and in verity set your claws upon the throat of Eve, and liberty to serve and reign at my side is thine!"

As she could not seem to die in the dunking stool, and as she could not live another day in the hell of bars and locks, Lilith purposed in her heart to give the fallen angel his desires, and try to escape his clutches on the outside, rather than the inside of her cage.

So she made effort to actually make love to Lucifer, who lay with her in the Broceliande Forest. A comfortable little cottage of stone became her new dwelling, and she wanted for nothing during her pregnancy.

When, in the twelfth month of the year, the child was delivered, Lilith and Lucifer called it Baphomet. The creature was male and female in one, possessing in equal measure the worst attributes of its parents, a horned, wicked thing from the beginning. Lilith instantly understood how Abel must have felt to look upon her.

"One hundred and one times I have sinned against creation," she lamented to the trees, strolling in the forest several paces ahead of the maid and manservants who governed the home on behalf of the Devil. But she held the unclean thing nevertheless, attempting to pour all the mothering of those who had perished into the abomination suckling upon her breast. "But also have I saved one hundred babies," she tried to reason with her sin. "Peradventure the Lord will look upon this and, knowing my heart, soften my sentence."

Hearing that she yet feared God and was not wholly possessed by and obsessed with the Devil (for he wanted nothing save to possess the whole of her being, day and night), envy caused the sneaking serpent to overstep. Lurking behind a tall oak, he hissed, "About that."

He walked straight up to Lilith and delicately took Baphomet into his arms, holding him in a soft, paternal manner for a moment and then handing him to the party of servants who had presently joined them in the wood.

"Your rebellion against me was vanity," he continued. Once started, he could not reverse his words. "For as you killed your seed, so too did the Sons of Cain take and kill theirs, learning that they could draw power from the suffering of the child, especially the male offspring. Your folly and their study greatly advanced the Sacred Sciences and will undoubtedly add great value in my plan to thwart His plan for the Ages."

"They all died?" The gray face was ashen.

"Two hundred babies, dead and laid to your charge, my wife. And there is more."

As Satan revealed the unmatched deception and dishonor with which he had defrauded her, Lilith was reborn, instantly remembering who she was. One hundred years of torture had nearly broken her, but the revelation of ongoing terror and murder of the innocent had revived the Otherworldly Being.

She had actually died in the cage, in the lake. The torture, rape, and imprisonment had killed the humanity in her, and only what spirit Azazel had given her remained in the half-mortal host. She was no longer any part mortal.

One of the braver shards of her personality clutched the green light behind her eyes and determined that *they* were not going to take it anymore. The gray skin became at once white again. And not only white: a shining, shimmering samite. The white hair gave way to the seductive raven's hue, and likewise did her black wings fill and blossom to former glory.

"What *more*?" the Primal Witch demanded.

"Adam and Eve have laid the murder of these infants at thy charge. They beseech God day and night that He might send Watchers to teach them."

"Teach them what?"

"Hunting." He was pleased with himself, having set in motion the very series of events that would cause Eve to seek out, and ultimately die whilst trying to kill, Lilith – whom he had wanted to slay Eve in the first place.

Lilith ascended twenty feet into the air, slowly and with regal authority and grace. "Let them hunt. I will reason with Eve. And if she will not harken unto my reason, I will become the monster they slanderously report me to be."

Noting that she was separating from their company, and seeing her full of strength and unsure he could stop her, Satan asked, "What of our child?"

Lilith spoke incantations that caused one manservant's head to explode, then another, then she fixed her red eyes upon the maidservant holding the Son of the Devil and his Concubine.

"Do not!" Lucifer cried.

"Let the sum be one hundred and one." She screeched and vanished above the trees, soaring above the primal forest.

Satan gathered the lifeless clump of swaddling, hooves, brains, and blood, cursing Lilith that he had no seed of his own, but pleased that he had activated his wife, hoping very much she would immediately seek an audience with Eve, doing the work of the plan in his stead.

Suddenly, Michael the Archangel appeared above the mourning father. "Your perversions have come before the Lord. To the Third Heaven you must," he commanded.

And Satan obeyed the command, returning to the Court of the Watchers and the Council of the Most High for a time, leaving men to prosper and Lilith as the lone terror roaming the countryside.

Chapter 8
The Days of Jared

From the beginning of the creation to the birth of Jared, son of Mahalaleel, was four hundred and ninety years. These were history's first seven generations. During this simple, pure and mostly golden era there were no incursions from the angels above, with the exception of the dread account of Lilith the Screech Owl, and the rogue villain Azazel.

As men began to multiply and spread quickly upon the earth, the tale of Lilith was first known as a shameful truth (for many were cowards, both regarding showing grace unto Lilith and attempting to rescue her for her mother's sake); then it became a tale of warning round the fire to the naughty and the wandering. At last it passed into legend.

Missing or harmed children were rare. Crime, disease, and hardship were scant.

Sin is a creeping thing, increasing by the ongoing replication of the flawed and dying blood of men. Men worsen by the generation. They do not improve like unto a fine wine, rather they stink of decay, as discarded fish, the long years in their mortal coils suffering the erosion of their fallen natures.

Man is not on an upward lift. He started high and fell.

He did not begin as a cave dweller, rather in well-designed abodes of wood and thatch from the start. And other than Adam and Eve when in their innocence, Man was ever clothed, mindful of modesty, never a rogue or violent, naked barbarian until oppression, tyranny, poverty, and governments made him so.

Though called a *fall,* and a fall it was, 'twas really at first a stumble, and then a diminishing. And Eve, whose husband was the original stumbler, possessed, like her faithful Adam, more character in the downy hair upon her earlobe than would a whole nation of the dregs living thirty generations thereafter.

Though no man is *good* whose deeds are weighed against the just demands of God, by relative scale were Adam and Eve good, as was the generation a good generation, for the better part, of good men. These walked with dragons and swam with the great sea monsters and were not afraid. They were blessed to see the Unicorn in his season and watch the Great Eagles fly fortunate travelers around the face of the middle earth.

The age was peaceful, not perfect; glad, but not without some mourning. Happy, but cautious.

And Eve, the queen, was above all, most cautious.

For Lilith remained. And roamed. And surely, in the wise of judgement of Eve, did still hunt and do deeds untold to innocent children.

***

Lilith emphatically did not hunt, neither do any foul or untoward deeds to the innocent. Rather she visited cruel and just death on the men who did these things, fully aware that she bore the burden of being accused of the very things she fought mightily to prevent.

***

A secret society had been formed by a fraction of men (numbering just nine, plus a few aspiring servants), each of whom was a descendent of Cain.

These venerated the dragon Tiamat as a fallen goddess and mourned her death in ritual, song, and offerings. They venerated the Screech Owl, Lilith, who was the consort, priestess and loving wife of their most high god. In their religious allegory, Lilith was driven from her lord by militant angels who sought to deny mankind the enlightenment and freedom that could have been theirs through the open rule of Lucifer, Lilith, and Baphomet, their son.

To give association to their gods by the beings or created things that they could see, Lucifer was symbolized by the sun, Lilith the dark moon, and Tiamat the life-giving seas.

Thus did this fellowship of men, this Order of the Dragon, turn rape into romance and villainy into virtue, developing a cult upon a foundation of lies. *They* abused small boys as they began to dabble in the Occult Sciences.

When a child would disappear, or the body thereof was discovered, the charge was laid to Lilith's account, even by those who, though lacking any other explanation, did not believe she existed. And Eve, failing to separate investigation from emotion, likewise did the same, ever conjuring thoughts, again and again, of Lilith seeking to seduce and lie with her husband.

Sitting at tea following a recent outrage, but one half-hour removed from holding a wailing mother, Eve, shaken by shock and fury, turned to Adam.

"We cannot another five hundred years of this suffer, my love. That we pass the day fishing, else painting, else weaving with no care for the morrow, neither the day, whilst a Night Hag takes our babes at will, is intentional blindness and formal injustice." A great, singular tear escaped, one breached dam being more forceful than a thousand droplets of minor rain, and made a slow 'S' shape as it navigated Eve's smooth cheek, at last disappearing into the golden torque about her neck, leaving a slight water stain upon her mortal covering, which was as pearl. "No matter if it happens once a year or once a decade. The loss of just one babe is one too many. Her talons must never another infant slash!"

Eve had asked her husband's permission, honoring that he was the one ultimately accountable for what might happen next. He did not agree, nor disagree, with his partner, but he did summarize. "We cannot find her. And when we see her, she is too swift for the fishnet, too strong for the hare's snare. Too wise for any device of mortals."

"Of mortals—" Eve started.

Adam gently interrupted. "Of mortals," he acquiesced, nodding. "But, my love, we have had nothing but misfortunate dealings with immortals." His failure in the Garden was as a great chain around his heart, pulling his very soul to the deepest abyss.

"Experience hath wrought wisdom, Bear." Eve called her husband after his favorite beast of the forest, hoping to encourage the greatly burdened ruler. "We are as old as they are." They laughed. "And will not be fooled again."

"A quiet heaven tends to mean a peaceful earth."

God was not entirely silent during this age, but He seemed to let early man live and learn and develop, as does a parent when a child matures. The Lord intervened and guided, but not to the negation of the free will of men. Still, the angels were created to glorify God and to minister unto men. When the relationship worked, angels taught men various good crafts and helped mortals understand how to effectively and efficiently work the land.

As Man had a tendency to worship the creation instead of the creator, and as angels had a tendency to want to hide God and draw worship to themselves, the Creator managed the matter *strategically and selectively.*

"They are supposed to help us," Eve pleaded. "Let the Watcher come down and show us how to hunt Lilith. To capture Lilith. To negotiate with Lilith. To make her stay away."

"Or to kill her." Adam said with his mouth what Eve said with her mind.

"If needs be, yes. But that is not what I want," she insisted. "I desire not to take the life of my daughter's daughter. I just want her to go away. For our kingdoms to be free of fear, at liberty when nighttime gives way to sleep."

Adam harkened to the desires of his wife. He rose from the table where the First Couple sat at tea, once again making decisions that would impact the lives that were now and every soul that would ever draw breath thereafter. He opened the door to the Watcher, who appeared in the form of a strikingly handsome young man, and directly requested the angel to intervene in the affairs of men.

Thus, by direct invitation from Adam himself did the Watchers come down into the world of men for to help them hunt, or capture, the Primal Witch in the Days of Jared.

Chapter 9
A Second Fall

Adam and Eve were beguiled again; again, subtly...

This time there was no manifestation of God Almighty, no proclamation of coming doom, no sentence of death and judgement. No ethereal serpents were de-winged and flattened to the dust this time.

God was silent.

The deception was slow – a step here, an inch there – and was born not, at the first, by conspiratorial grand design, but by a slow, burning lust.

Lust for adoration.

Lust for veneration.

Lust for the most peculiar and fair of all of God's creation: the daughters of men.

Adam had beseeched the Watchers to teach men how to hunt the Primal Witch. And the Watchers, known by many names in prose and song, who are the Titans of old, did take advantage of their summonses, and quickly develop a fondness for direct adoration from the mortals, and for women.

Azazel was the captain of these Watchers. He already had a good rapport amongst the first generation of men, who were now elders, teaching many of them how to keep sheep and cattle and bring forth crops. Some may have recognized him as connected to the mischief of five centuries ago, but not conclusively, and neither God nor angel made the identity of Luluwa's rapist and murderer known to Adam and Eve.

He manifested most often as a very tall man, softening the fright and awe of a Host of Heaven, and did give as his name *Prometheus*, by which he is known by the bards in poetry and lore.

Under the pretext of hunting the witch (all the while knowing that the might of men could not slay her, neither the cunning of men bring her down) did he introduce metallurgy: the fashioning of every kind of short and long weapon. Also, he taught them archery and the lethal use of slings and catapults, and the ways of killing the fowls of the air (and in theory, a flying she-devil). Additionally, men were given the knowledge of how to hide spikes in a walking path, to set diverse, cruel traps using strings, metal hooks, and levers. The foundational and working knowledge of war-waging was herein established.

Azazel did more than provide the inanimate objects; he quickened the blade by *teaching peaceful men how to strike and slash as killers*. Temperate men became crazed with confidence when knowing how to thrust a spear, and self-controlled men forgot themselves when given advanced skills on how to crush, dislocate, and maim.

But the end of this knowledge was vanity, for when Lilith was, from time to time, located, she was too swift, too fierce, and too much for Man's first armed (and armored) warriors. When agitated after a physical encounter, as a big cat tires at being pawed upon by kittens, she would swat the mortals away, then change tactic and use the power of words to finish them. Lilith had achieved mastery of a magick borne within, and with it could splatter the heads of ten men through the wrinkling of her nose.

That Azazel surely had known this *before* he gave unto men weapons and delusions of grandeur became evident to Adam and Eve. Alas: *too late*. He was mischievous, often without an apparent cause. Their concern grew, but on balance did not outweigh their desperate need, for Lilith, now agitated, could not be curtailed.

Azazel had achieved nothing on behalf of Man for killing the monster, and everything on behalf of Man for killing one another, and ever seeking his counsel and direction on how to do, or avoid doing, the same. In this did the Goat God relish and revel.

But metallurgy and martial arts were not the ends of his dealings. For above all else did Azazel lust after women. He fantasized obsessively two-hundred-score times a day over his cruel encounters with Luluwa, insatiably hungry for when he might again enjoy the flower of a daughter of Adam.

Lust and addiction love company.

To this end, Azazel, fearing that Michael might descend and make the villain known to the world, or bind him from interacting with his adoring devotees, tempered temporarily his cravings by seeing men indulge theirs. He gave to women the arts of how they could paint their eyes and nails, alter the color of their hair, enhance the shades and depth of their faces with fats and oils and dyes, and adorn themselves with enticing apparel that gave them immeasurable power over helpless men, whose lust over their comely presentations drove many to distraction.

To wield a sword and be seen at the feat with a regal, sensual, painted lady upon one's elbow, doing erotic and dark deeds in the bedchamber: this for the common man was heaven on earth. And the heavenly being that introduced the same was worthy of worship.

Indeed, men worshipped Prometheus, the Old Goat God, the Cloven Hoof, and the Old Goat God used every occasion to look upon the wives and damsels he had fashioned, scheming and plotting for a way to lie with them. As all this unfolded and the culture shifted, changed and developed, his primary commission remained incomplete.

Lilith yet lived.

And while Lilith lived, a great portion of men upon the earth increasingly and unwittingly worshipped her father, bowing down to the very one who had given them so much calamity in the first place.

***

When Adam and Eve congressed with the Watchers, they met near the base of the most prestigious mountain in the center of the middle earth, a place that would later be called *Mount Hermon,* which is by interpretation *The Mountain of Desecration.* To Adam and Eve it was the highest peak known, and it fondly recalled to them the City of God, when the Lord dwelt with them prior to Adam's transgression.

To the deceitful Watchers it had the same similitude with a more sinister reverence. For here could they meet and feign in their corrupt hearts ruling from the Holy Mount over their subjects, the mortals, below.

To the summit of Hermon did the First Couple ascend, there to declare grievances against their servant-become-meddler-become-god.

"I demand an end to this vanity, whose end is emptiness and death." Adam chastised the angel. "Little boys fear their eyes to shut, and mothers fret to exhaustion to a lad's eighth year."

The Mother of all the Living was aflame with righteous anger and contempt, adding, "While your men frolic and thrust upon the silly and the shallow. You have raised no army, and have compounded the sorrow of our Age."

Azazel started to make his retort, but was interrupted by the dramatic manifestation of another angel, bathed in light and every precious jewel. The light was blinding, and when it abated, lo: the angel was a man of above thirty years with short black hair and brilliantly dark blue (or black, for the color could not be discerned) eyes. He wore no beard, and his visage was as chiseled marble; muscular cheeks and jowls, a pointed chin in perfect symmetry with the land's end of his thin nose, which had the slightest upward turn at the tip. Four and six tenths' cubits tall and hovering above his audience another eight cubits, the robed visitor was as a white column let down straight from heaven.

Adam and Eve should have recognized the angel but did not.

"Prometheus has meant well, but defeat has discouraged him, allowing him to be…" The shimmering being looked through the First Couple, beyond Azazel and down the slope to where people dwelt in ornate yet simple villas below. Eyes clearly fixed upon fair damsels, he continued, "…distracted."

"Cannot he who is indicted answer to the charge?" Adam demanded, wanting Prometheus to speak for himself.

"Sometimes one who is too close to the fire becomes blinded by the flame," the angel answered, recovering his lustful gaze and half agape snarl, restoring the original form of his stoic, marble face. "My station is higher than this ministering spirit. He has brought much light unto the world of men, but alas is too close to the matter. If you stay upon the present course, you shall in no wise defeat the menacing little white owl."

Eve, having gained five centuries of intuition, gave passing notice to the pet name and apparent affection directed towards the she-devil, but dismissed it as implausible on account of the beauty and holiness of the divine messenger. "Has the Lord sent thee?"

"I come in the name of the god of this world," came the reply. "Lilith is too strong for your mightiest, too swift for your arrows, too smart for the most cunning of your traps. No man can defeat her. Added to this, she is full of a dark force from birth, such that not even Behemoth or Leviathan can stand against her."

As the Holy One represented himself as an emissary from God Himself, hope rushed out of Eve; the unflappable queen began to quake, her eyes to well.

"No creature fashioned by God can slay her, it is true," the messenger went on. "But there might be a way." Here did the shining visitor descend, touching down upon the mount, taking Eve by the hand. "Perhaps only an unnatural thing can dispose of an unnatural thing?"

Adam removed the angel's gentle clasp upon his wife's hand, standing as a strong wall between them. "You would answer one sin against nature with another?"

"Your God certainly did not smite Lilith dead, neither is He here now to speak against the hope of this plan. If He does not reckon it evil, and if a great good should a little evil beget, how speak you against it?"

Adam responded, "Nature itself tells us that animals multiply after their own kind. The horse does not lie with the cow."

"Am I not so much in the similitude of a man that your analogy falls short? Though the glory of my body differs from yours, does not one star differ from another, yet of the same kind? He created us with the ability to bring forth seed, yet there are no women amongst the Elect, and only the Moon as the queen over the luminaries."

Adam reasoned within himself for a moment, then challenged the heavenly visitor. "We do not know what God might have done, for by my grave sin the whole creation fell. He may have made you counterparts in the world to come, or had some other intention. The Father keeps His own counsel on this mystery, and we must deal with where we are, and what we are doing. This is an unnatural recommendation. Are you sure God sent y—?"

"Bear. Enough, please," Eve pleaded. "I cannot suffer one more child to meet some cruel, ritual death at the hands of Lilith. Philosophy be damned, let us try what he proposes, I beseech you!"

***

Lilith killed no children.

She did not haunt their dreams. She did not make off with them in the dark and dreary night. Lilith only hunted the Order, the sons of Cain who practiced untold debauchery and wickedness upon the innocent.

Yet Adam and Eve, the federal heads of all forming proto-kingdoms on the earth, did consider allowing the procreation of demigods, that one might arise and smite her.

***

Adam loved his wife; he cherished her above all things: esteem and respect without bounds. Giving the final words of protest ere a husband's consent to plans they cannot endorse but for love's sake support anyhow, he asked, "And if one arises that is threefold worse than she, who will kill it?"

The relevance and veracity of Adam's question notwithstanding, the couple reached accord with the angel that the Watchers might *make* a being to match and defeat the Primal Witch.

***

Azazel adjourned to the Second Heaven, there to await further instruction.

"Take thyself, and two besides, and the three of you go down and take wives of the daughters of men." Satan relished in his work, finding that Eve was as beautiful as when he had first met her: strong-willed, passionate, intense… and gullible.

Chapter 10
Atlantis

"And it came to pass, when men began to multiply on the face of the earth, and daughters were born unto them, That the sons of God saw the daughters of men that they were fair; and they took them wives of all which they chose."

Genesis 6:2

Azazel worked exhaustively to coerce and convince the first three Watchers, finally gaining their consent to the pact. Their consciences warned them that the deed was a violation of the creation itself and would bring about inconceivable punishment.

In the end, the Goat agreed by solemn covenant to bear the full weight and consequence for whatever may come of the rebellion, serving as a propitiation for the sins of his kindred, a substitutionary stand-in for every guilty occupant of heavenly places. Just as Adam was identified as the federal head of all humanity, Azazel became the accountable representative of all of the angelic realm.

Through Adam, corruption and death passed to all men by reason of his sin.

Through Azazel, corruption passed to the angels by reason of his rebellion.

The start of the First Incursion was nothing like the vile assault visited on Princess Luluwa. The angels manifested as men, wooing the damsels as would a farmer, builder, or artisan. The Holy Ones married women and made consensual love in normal fashion as would a husband and wife. There was no violence or fear of the angels, save the fact that the first

Fallen Ones were Titans, and even clothed in the semblance of men, were so tall and mighty that some women did perish when giving birth, on account of the offspring being too large to safely pass through the birth canal.

The early days of the plot to manufacture a champion to best Lilith reminded Eve, seeing it unfold (and knowing how it must end), of when a curious camel pokes its nose into a tent. First just the nose enters, rooting around and puffing with snort-filled inquisitiveness. The children in the tent gleefully laugh, petting the camel's snout, and mind not that pots are spilled, a vase is broken and the clothes basket is overturned. The nose is comely, and the head is adorable.

But the neck follows the head. The tent cannot accommodate the large, twisting, animated tree trunk exploring the circumference of the small abode. Laughter gives way to dismay as soon everything is broken, the flaps of the wall are breached, and the tethers and pins themselves are creaking and protesting, barely clinging to the dirt floor where they anchor the home.

Lastly, the hump enters and the curious camel stands aright. The tent itself is uprooted… and no more.

This is what Eve witnessed as the beings above became infatuated, obsessively enamored with the women below. What was three angels became two hundred, and from there increased to a multitude of foolish servants of the Most High God who forsook their heavenly estates, trading paradise above for the earthly pleasures of the flesh below. Lust ran amuck.

Lust has an ever companion, which is the thirst for power. Sex and power are as two great pillars of every strong kingdom that rises… and falls.

The Fallen Ones established a governance structure and began to implement in earnest the first kingdoms upon the face of the earth.

A Watcher is not a kind of angel. A Watcher is an *office*, created by God Himself prior to the Fall, anticipating a symbiotic and collegial relationship between Man – who was to rule – and angel – who was to rule in a subordinate role, serving and assisting Man. To this end, the Watchers, who became memorialized in song, legend, and lore as Titans, were comprised of representatives from across the spectrum of God's Heavenly Host, be they Dominions, Thrones, Powers, Principalities, fiery Seraph or Cherubs.

The Titans, or *Old Gods*, responsible for the incursion numbered six. In heaven they had shared positions of authority with eighteen others, with Michael and Lucifer making two sets of twelve, or twenty-six, for God's number for governance is twelve.

Coveting a likeness to God, and wanting to multiply their ambitions to procreate a heaven on earth, the Primal Six 'created' six goddesses who joined the Titans as Titanesses.

After this manner were wrought the goddesses of old: the Titans married mortal daughters and caused them to be with child. If the offspring was female, a half-angel, half-mortal female, the Titan would impregnate their own daughter just as soon as she was of childbearing age, bringing forth a being who was but one-fourth of the seed of men. Six of these were elevated to the role of Titaness, the eldest granddaughters of the gods.

The twelve Titans were considered *Generation Zero*, beginning their transformation of the world that was in the Days of Jared, four hundred and ninety years from the Beginning; five hundred and ninety-six years before the birth of Noah, they multiplied their progeny upon the face of the earth.

The first generation born immediately after the Titanesses were created included cyclopes and giants who were as tall as the cedar tree, girthy as the oak. Zeus, the mightiest of the first generation of gods, and the heroes of old were born at this time.

The Titans developed two major centers of government; one in what would become, after the Flood, known as Olympus, the other from the infamous Mount Hermon itself. These were the Holy Mounts of the gods from which flowed ten regions, administered in turn by ten territorial rulers, but the ten were subordinate to the two, again making twelve.

Both God and Satan were quiet in this age, two opponents in silent, stoic contemplation; each confidently pondering strategy, calmly considering maneuvers, letting the lesser pawns manage for a time by themselves.

Chapter 11
Men Are the Problem

Although the Watchers who disobeyed their office were given to corruption, lust, greed, and gross misuse of their gifts and knowledge, the first of their progeny were not so.

Most of them, with a few villainous exceptions, were kind, charitable, and moral. They loved mankind and had a curiosity and fascination for the silent One True God, whose name was decreasingly called upon, who was still known yet unknown, who was vanishing from the thoughts and concerns of men; a remnant of the Patriarchs like Adam, Seth and Enos notwithstanding.

It is speculated that the pantheon of heroes and Olympians retained the virtuous bits of Man, passed on to them from their mortal mothers, which caused the goodness of Man to press upon their conscience, compelling them to reign and conduct themselves justly.

But this is folly, for Man is not good.

The first generation of gods was heroic, just and virtuous because of the angelic portions within them, consistent with the Elect of God who remained faithful to the Most High. In this regard they were different from their direct parents, but not different from their kind.

The more of the fallen, sinful, and dying blood of Man mixed with angel, the more the good bits of heaven gave way to vile and nasty ingredients of men below.

The Titans fell by their own accord the moment they chose to make a binding covenant that they would marry the daughters of Adam. In their pride they began to make a boastful show to their women of the machines they could smith, the crafts they could devise, and the cities they could erect. But though they sought to be like the Most High, none had an original thought, for the created can never be as the Creator. Instead, they could only mimic or pervert that which already was. To this end they made constant forgeries of the City of God: its temple, its garden, its stones of fire. First atop Mount Hermon and Olympus, then on mounts and in groves throughout the world.

The Titans were corrupt. Men are corrupt. The repetitive blending of the Titans and then the offspring of the Titans with corrupt men begat increasingly extreme corruption. But between these, as one thin layer of red silt in a vase of white sand, were the Olympians and heroes, which were not corrupt.

And these held regard for the agreement with Adam and Eve to subdue Lilith (whom they knew not was the victim of above five hundred years of false witness); to do the work for which they had been *created*.

***

Now Zeus was the eldest son by the captain of the Titans, Cronos. Cronos was subject only to Azazel, and Azazel subject only to Lucifer, and Lucifer was in exile, else locked in bonds in the Third Heaven.

Cronos fathered twelve children; Zeus was the eldest, Poseidon the youngest.

The brothers were born in the likeness of men: identical in height at four and one-half cubits (which is a foot-length taller than an average man); identical in marbled, perfect form; identical in curly hair and, by the age of fourteen, short, straight, perfect beards.

Zeus's eyes were pale blue and his hair golden. Poseidon's eyes were fluorescent turquoise outlined in diamonds, and his hair as the algae in the shallow parts of the sea.

The Titans, by reason of jealousy and malice, loathed the gods, and a clash of the Titans simmered to a low boil. Yet with war upon the horizon, the Olympians prioritized having counsel with the First Couple, hoping to honor them in word and deed.

Adam and Eve possessed a small wooden dwelling near where Abel and Luluwa had dwelt. Additionally, they lodged in a cave very near the eastmost gates of Eden. Daily for seven months and then weekly for seventy years, Eve had approached the gates of Eden, falling at the feet of the sword-wielding guardians who kept a perpetual post ensuring none could approach the Garden and its two famous trees, least of all Adam and Eve. There she would beg for God's forgiveness from sunrise to sunset, then rest in the coolness of the cave, renewing her repentance next morning.

Although Man had forsaken God in the Garden, God did not forsake Man. Through the agency of the Cherubs did God try and console Eve, promising that she would be restored to the Garden in the fullness of time.

"How long?" she would appeal with eyes that could form no more tears, yet somehow found more, and a body shaken with regret, a heart broken with contrition. "How long until I am restored to my garden, my city and my Lord?"

The heavenly keeper would hand the sword of flame to his watchmate, stoop, and meet Eve upon the dirt, embracing her. The answer, never said coldly but never changing, was: "For six days shalt ye labor, and on the seventh day enter into His rest."

And the days of the Lord are as a thousand years.

As time passed, Eve stopped groveling. Once she reached her eightieth decade, she dwelt in the cave as a periodic ritualistic and nostalgic reminder of her transgression (as a man revisits the tavern where he lost his first love, or a mother to the tearoom where a quarrel cost her a grown daughter) and to enjoy the beauty of creation, looking forward to its restoration, but never quite loosing the knots of pain tethering her to what had been.

Eve's repentant sorrow could never be fully consoled. She had brought death and grief, and worse, her actions had led to the things contrary to the order of God's creation itself. Eve reckoned herself the real *Mother of Monsters*.

As another punitive reminder of her failings, she and her husband now met, near the spot of her transgression, the monsters that walked the earth as a result of her sin. These were very handsome monsters, she noted.

There, under the mist of a bright, sun-filled day just beyond the reach of Paradise, Adam, the First Man, the one who had walked with God Himself upon the fertile, rich soils of the garden of life, who had named the beast of the fields, classified their kind, raced with jaguars and played with apes, the one blessed enough to be a spectator of the Lord Himself wrestling with dragons for pleasure, looked up at Zeus… and marveled.

Poseidon initiated the discourse, offering words of adoration and praise, but his words were quickly cut off by Eve, who had no taste for pageantry with her otherworldly guests.

"Three days ago," she began, "a cyclops obtained a high-ground position over her, assuming she was trapped below in a canyon without pathway for escape." Eve need not utter the name for all gathered to understood who 'she' was. "A twinkling of the eye later, she had severed the cyclops's arm cleanly at the joint. And fed the thing its own arm!" Desperation overcame royalty, and the High Queen of the Living cursed the sky. "It at once choked to death and bled out, and she had expended no more vigor than doth a sloth when crossing the way!"

"My Lady—" Poseidon tried to speak but gave way, for an angry woman is more frightful than any god.

"If none of you can stand against her, then is not the very existence of your entire race in vain, and your continuation folly? Ought not the lot of you cast yourselves into the sea, that all the gods drown!"

"But Poseidon is Lord of the Sea, and the construct of the chambers of his chest give him breath beneath the waves, like unto the great whales." Zeus interceded, paused, raised an eyebrow, and laughed.

"I will find a more comprehensive analogy to explain your collective demise," Eve retorted, her distress eased by the king of the gods. She permitted herself a laugh as well.

As did Adam, the unusual congress of legends in unison.

"That you are kind, fair and quite unlike your parents is reported throughout the land," Eve acknowledged. "Forgive my angry words. Come, sit at mead in our cave."

Adam and Eve's dwelling would come to be called the *Cave of Treasures*, for it contained relics from the beginning of time, including the first coats of skins the Lord God had prepared for them prior to their expulsion from Eden. The Olympians asked to see these and like items of significance, showing great curiosity over what life had been like at the dawn of history, and great empathy for the tragic centuries of Adam and Eve. Zeus could clearly see that the death of every child, the night terror of every lad weighed upon Eve with such regret and radical personal responsibility that he wondered how the guilt had not brought her to her grave.

Mead was consumed. Relics viewed. Kindness and collaboration restored. Eve returned to the matter at hand.

Lilith.

"Of a truth, what can you do? Is Lilith to be a dark goddess over all of us?" She was more polite, but no less intense.

Zeus sat upon a bench, delicately twisting his powerful hands in opposite motions around a spear (Adam claimed it to be the first spear created. Boys love spears and swords, and in this regard, Zeus, too, was a lad.); he was not holding it as a weapon, but rather as a bar or rod. *And many rods, bent and fastened, become as a cage.*

"The Old Gods tell of a cage that can hold her." Zeus carefully placed the artifact against the wall of the dwelling, then allowed his eyes to pass over a net, also the first of its kind. "The legends suggest that it is enchanted, and that once contained it arrests her power so that she can be—"

"Run through!" Eve offered, now herself looking at the old spear.

"Reasoned with." Zeus had no illusions about the difficulty of actually slaying Lilith, if the Primal Witch could even be slain. "I do not presume to be able to vanquish her, but my brother and I may have the strength to force her into the cage."

"If it exists," Adam pointed out. "If it were as easy as returning her to a charmed prison cell, surely the Watchers would have quickly done this, that they could return to their fornication and be freed of our constant requests that they honor their oaths."

"Prometheus is so preoccupied with the fornication that you speak of that he cares for nothing else, save how many women he can take in the field or abduct from the pond. He is wanton and mad. And I cannot pretend to assume the motives of madman... or angel." Zeus clearly hated Azazel, and this endeared the God of Thunder to Eve, whose hatred was white-hot for the same foe.

"The cage is real." Poseidon joined the discourse, emphatic about what he had learned. "A league of men conceal it. These are the first order of priests, the sons of Cain. They are the merchants of dark sciences that they learned from—" The God of the Sea looked towards the heavens, though it was not yet midday.

"From your parents above." Eve's sense of direct disdain over the activities from the heavenly realm that had forever redirected the course of the earthly resumed.

"What motive would men have to guard the one thing that might bring hope in foiling the huntress that punishes our land and scourges our children?" asked Adam of the very same heavens. "Why would men conceal the one weapon that can bind the one killing our babies? What motive have they?"

Chapter 12
"Show Them"

Zeus and his kin faced threat and tribulation on three fronts. War to overthrow their corrupt parents was imminent; a secret society of mortals was possibly in league with Lilith, or wanted to hold power for some unknown purpose over her cage; and the Screech Owl herself continued to butcher the giants who hunted her.

Moreover, the incursion against creation was increasing, the interbreeding of angel and man no longer limited to two hundred Watchers. The luminaries also suspended their rotations, periodically leaving heaven to find love and sensuality, then hastening back sneakily to their courses above, choosing to be delusional in pretending that *He* hadn't seen, or wouldn't notice.

The exponents of this mischief increased the variety and oddity of beings upon the earth. And surely factions and new races and kindreds would arise. Zeus was in no wise immune to the allure of woman, and himself fell to the temptation, begetting many sons and daughters himself, chief amongst them being Apollos.

The authority in Heaven continued its silence (from the perspective of Man), and the earth was a haven of gods and monsters.

***

Then God spoke to Uriel, a faithful Watcher, a Seraph by kind and of the company and friendship of the archangels Michael and Gabriel, and the very guardian who wielded the flaming sword, saying: "Show them."

***

One is the number of unity, for God is one.

Three is number of deity, for God is three, and all strong relationships are triune in nature, mirroring God, who is three.

Twelve is the number of governance. The earth has four corners, and all rulers thereof should develop and maintain the strongest of bonds and relationships with their citizens, representing the goodness of God unto them. Thus, four times three is twelve.

Seven is the number of perfection, for in seven days did God create the cosmos and the earth, which is the center of His creation. On the seventh day did God rest, seeing that His creation was good.

Seven are the virtues and characteristics of God, and the virtues of His assemblies or churches through the Ages. For the Lord is all in all. And seven is God's favorite number.

Nine is the number of divine completion or sovereignty, for God is three, and three times three is nine.

And the stars themselves declare the purposes of God in numbers, as does the earth and the sky in geometry.

Seven angels did God set aside as favored, loyal and blessed. And Michael was the captain of these, but Uriel was God's favorite, being called seventh.

The Lord once asked Uriel, in the moments following the catastrophe in the Garden, "Surely thou wilt never betray me?"

"The sword Thou hast forged for me and the breath of life Thou breathed into the chambers of my bosom shalt serve Thee in every generation, O God," answered the Seraph, who when not clothed in the appearance of a man appeared as a shining serpent blanketed in six ginormous wings. Each was twice as long as his body, the width of each half the height of his body. Spectacular and peculiar, the other angels mused that this type of Seraph, whose feathers were made of fire (for there is another kind, which has a translucid, fluid, milky body covered with eyes), was 'all wings and thus could not manage to hold the tabret, or the harp'.

Though light-natured and full of humor, returned to the other Hosts in kind, Uriel could also assume a very serious disposition. He was the judgement and fear of the Lord personified, and in accord given many tasks.

First, he was made to join the Watchers, but was surely not amongst those who sinned. The Seraph's charges included ministering to the repentant, comforting the sorrowful, and teaching sciences, poetry, and justice.

He was also a custodian: the keeper of the keys to a secret place that God made for the Devil and his angels.

When the Watchers witnessed God fix the foundations of the earth upon its pillars after the fourth day of creation, they celebrated in song, shouting and singing to the glory of the Creator. They were blessed in witnessing, and even participating in, the final garnishing and stabilizing of the raw lump of clay that was the created order; blessed to directly see the Lord prepare it to be inhabited, used and enjoyed.

But they were never meant to be its stewards, and their prince above all things detested the seemingly torturous and intentional paradox of being made such principal participants of something that was fashioned for others. For how did this differ from the master having his hounds achieve the hunt, only to give the fowl to his cat… in the presence and company of his dogs?

The Watchers watched much, but not all. They saw the pillars; they saw the foundation stones. They understood that the Deep's waters outside the world flowed in and out from below the firmament, aided by the work of two great dragons and four angels.

But God concealed one realm from the Heavenly Hosts. Knowing the beginning from ending and anticipating their rebellion, the Lord God created Tartarus, the land of the dead, even before death was a notion in the mind of angel or man.

Tartarus was uniquely structured to hold both ethereal bodies and bodies made of celestial flesh. Dead men and living angels could equally traverse the Underworld. Regions and parts were as paradise – a kingdom of rest and peace for the righteous, awaiting the day when God would undo Adam's transgression and clothe men in new flesh to operate a restored, new earth. Elsewhere were special caverns, palaces and compartments designed for specific individuals foreordained to glory or to shame, based upon the foreknowledge of the Creator.

Next was a void and intentional nothing deep beneath the earth. An abyss of countless utter darkness.

And last of all was Hell. The place of torment and punishment created for the Watchers whom God knew would one day leave the Third Heaven and commit wickedness, violating the cosmos, the earth, the seed of mankind; molesting and traumatizing history itself, contributing ruin to the generations of men.

Hell was not created for men, and it is contrary to God's will and purpose that any lost soul suffer damnation. Indeed, every unbeliever who makes the woeful journey to the Country of the Damned is an uninvited guest.

A lake of fire burned there perpetually, a wide, expansive border between Hell and the less foreboding compartments of Tartarus. The body of brimstone and lava was so vast that the natural eye could not see from shore to shore, the intensity of the heat so great that a resident in Hell would inhale nothing save sulfur night and day. No words ever penned by the oracles, neither sung by the bards, can properly articulate the horrors of Hell.

And Uriel, whom the poets conflate with other gods and personalities, nominating him *Hades*, was placed as guardian of the Gates of Hell: the main surface entrance located at the base of the mountain which is called Hermon.

***

The Seraph descended upon the two distracted Olympians, who were talking over each other as waves compete to crash upon the tide's shore. Making their return from the Cave of Treasures to Olympus, the distressed gods were trying to solve the young world's problems and were caught unawares by the orb of glory that landed lightly in front of them, then unfolded its wings, speaking with a voice that rattled as the whisper of the wind upon the reeds, but in tone low and masculine, full of command and control.

The gods were awestruck, wanting to fall in fear (as men do) before the messengers of the Most High.

"Fear not," said Uriel. "Troubles have you many, but I am sent to help you solve one of them. Or," he laughed, "at least show you where to store them."

Zeus and Poseidon possessed no understanding of what the angel might mean by his words, nor an inkling of where he might take them, but they knew his authority was somehow authentic – somehow greater than that of even Cronos, whom a myriad of men bowed before and worshipped.

To the entry of the Gates of Hell he brought the Olympians, then issued grave warning.

"From the beginning were the bars of these gates made to contain fallen angels. The iron will paralyze the corrupt properties that animate their spirit, rendering them weak nigh unto death. Touch neither gate nor shackle, for I know not whether the mortal parts of you will make them harmless, or if you will suffer endless and unyielding agony." Uriel spoke with sincerity, having only theories about the composition of the interbred wonders before him. "Moreover," he continued, "an angel is a spirit with a celestial body, which differs from the flesh of men and beasts, whose spirits live in earthen vessels. Their bodies—" He paused, correcting himself somewhat, for Uriel too was an angel. "*Our* bodies are heavenly and constituted to traverse all the four realms. Heaven, earth, the Deep… and the world below, where I will now take you. Whether *your* bodies will descend safely down the chutes and into the pits, I know not. You may burst asunder, ignite as a flint to driftwood, or glide peacefully as one of my kind. The risk is yours."

The Lord of the Sea and the Master of the Mists considered the words – weighty words.

Poseidon knew by experience that he could survive in the deepest ocean, and the bottom of a great pond was as refreshing to his lungs as was a morning climb in the high hills to others. Zeus could fly as the birds and ascend above the canopy of paradisical mist that irrigated the lush greens of the fertile lands below. Like unto the fowls of the air, he could enjoy observing the wonders of creation through the prism of sunshine filtering through the canopy of vapor and mist that covered the earth. Alternatively, he could in an instant drop to a lower elevation and enjoy the clearest blue skies and the direct brightness and glory of the sun.

Both gods, being gods, were confident nigh unto arrogance; but the prospect of descending to the Undiscovered Country frightened them. They knew what they could do, but didn't know what their bodies *could not do,* for there was no scripture, oracle or sage wisdom about the capacities and limitations of beings that were not supposed to exist in the first place.

Afraid, but knowing that Cronos and the eleven had overt designs to kill the Olympians (Zeus and Poseidon continued to lack understanding of what that meant as well. Lilith had slain many cyclopes and not a few giants. *Did they have a soul? Where did the soul go? What does it mean to kill an abomination?*) and replace them with children more aligned with their insatiable appetite for bloodlust and tyrannical control over creation, they decided to hazard the risk and travel with Uriel to the world below.

The fiery serpent, Uriel, opened the gates, and escorted the two famous gods down to Hell.

Precious angels, faithful and unwavering, could be seen along the way. They served as guardians, being permanent fixtures in a maze of iron doors, hidden passageways, vaults, and thousands of gates and ominous dark towers. *If like unto their kindred, these dutiful spirits must live in perpetual agony, being so near to and surely interacting with the purity of the Maker's Special Iron,* Poseidon thought.

As God had formed the creation by his words, the creative and authoritative power of the words spoken by Uriel compelled the angels to give way, to stand down, or open the vaults and doors at each segment of the journey.

And herein is the origin of magick, which is the understanding of the power of words and how that they compel spirits to act, and the perversion or misuse thereof.

"Mark the commands, and know them," Uriel ordered. "For I will not be here when you bind the Twelve."

And Poseidon, awestricken by the whole of the experience (Zeus was more stoic, and did not favor being below the surface. He listened whilst praying silently to whatever being might hear him to hasten the conclusion of the Seraph's tour and lesson), carefully marked the words, down to pitch and inflection, fascinated by how the angels responded to their power.

The gods noted that Tartarus was formed not like unto the mountains and valleys, or the striking natural beauty of God's gardens, but rather like the ramparts of the temples atop Hermon or Olympia: full of stonework, architecture, dowels, and steel. God Himself was the mason of the kingdom below the Earth, an actual series of cities amongst enclaves and streams of lava. Tessellated flooring, black marble framed and outlined in gold, and ornate stonework was present throughout. There was dark beauty in the Underworld, and the artistic and intentional use of torches and lanterns (oiled by angels, else by some force unknown to the Olympians) revealed vast, high ceilings decorated with so many star maps that the ceilings of Hell matched the ceiling of Earth and the floorboards of Heaven. There were lakes, lagoons, and barges that could ferry two hundred souls, the bows shaped as curving dragons, lions, or swans.

The subterranean paradise bordered a vast gulf, the bottom of which could not be measured, and across the gulf, Hell awaited the unlikely troop.

What was dark, eerie, and striking instantly transitioned to terrible, even on the good side of the border of the abyss. Fear itself seemed to rise as a steam from the gulf and impose its air on the visitors. *If it is already this oppressive, what happens when we are over there?* Zeus struggled to breathe, as did the Lord of the Sea, and they now both longed for the ordeal to be over, to turn, to run, to flee.

Poseidon could swim but not fly. His brother turned to Uriel, who was as a living torch and already lightly flapping his wings, making ready to cross over into Hell. Showing the bravery and courage that would cement Zeus's fame, the most renowned and popular of all gods, the Olympian put away his fear and substituted it with perfectly timed jest.

"Will those feathers actually burn my brother?" He smiled. "Or are they just for a grandiose divine show to dazzle children and petrify men?"

Uriel descended back to level ground with his guests, closing his wings and dimming the light given by his fiery feathers. With the sternest, most judgmental look that a serpentine being can cast (for snakes have natural smiles and have to force a gruff expression), he responded in a rushy, hollow voice. "Zeus..."

The king of the gods stepped back, hoping to not be cast into the abyss by his holy host. He didn't respond but rather broadened his stance, readying for anything.

"Have you ever smelled roasted fish?"

Zeus didn't know what to say.

Poseidon absolutely knew not what to say.

Five seconds that were as five centuries passed in silence – and the Watcher laughed a slithery, wet, snakey laugh.

His laugh gave the gods license to laugh, but Poseidon still wondered if he might be cooked, by accident or for Uriel's now exposed predisposition for humor, during the flight.

The Holy Angel whisked up the Sea God from underneath the pit of his arms with no more effort than a mother gathers a basket of kittens, and conveyed him over the abyss that lies betwixt paradise and the darkest hell, setting him safely, and unscorched, upon the surface of the outer rim.

Poseidon, overwhelmed by the pungency of the Lake of Fire, which he could smell but did not see, only noted a few features of this region of Tartarus, for such was the darkness and thickness of despair that his shoulders pulled forward, causing him to plod along, hunched, in a sort of saddened trance. Zeus forged along in the same condition. He did see a system of crystal chutes and passages built into the walls and cavernous ceilings and, at their destination, a great cauldron with still water resting at the bottom of the final chute.

Uriel was aware that Poseidon studied the cauldron, pipes, and chutes, and that he was curious and confused. He explained very little, only offering, "It allows them to see the world above."

Flames flickered here and there, seeming both random and by design, as were pools of lava. Very near to the cauldron were empty iron cages, dangling, menacing, and sorrowful. Intricate machines of torture and punishment, they were hung as chandeliers by chains whose starting points could not be seen, disappearing into the darkness above. Within the cells were hooks and spikes, and it was self-evident that they would close upon the prisoner in such a manner that as he moved, layers of flesh would be removed in the opposite direction. Tall spikes were positioned so that the prisoner would be impaled through his hinder parts should he yield to fatigue and, resting his legs, assume a sitting position.

In this part of Hell, these prisons for the chiefs of the rebellion numbered eleven.

What of the twelfth cage? Zeus asked with his eyes. He could count but little else, for the air of judgement did cause the god's knees to knock, and a persistent faint feeling made overmuch conversation impossible.

Uriel answered the unspoken query, saying, "Azazel has his own special place."

The Elect Angel summonsed one of his own and, taking a large leather scrip from him, in turn passed it to Zeus. The contents were cuffs of iron, made specifically to bind Titans, making them too weak and, once shackled, drowsy, and incapacitated, easy to transport from the surface above to their containers for future judgement.

"Wage your war against your parents, and when opportunity is won, here in prison bind them. Unless they repent of their folly, no flesh will survive that is not corrupted, and nothing redeemable will remain upon the earth."

Zeus and Poseidon, filled with the fear of God, understood that He was not silent; He was very active in His own courts, and His patience and longsuffering were waning.

The Olympians, who were also beings of lust and naughtiness but whose conscience and capacity for love and justice dueled within them (and each of their siblings were burdened with the same duality), were given direct witness to the creative power and some of the unfolding purposes of the Most High.

They would seek to overthrow the debauched Titans, then hope God would look upon them, though not part of His creation, though reproaches and walking symbols of sin, and show mercy, avoiding an inheritance of eternal damnation in the Lake of Fire.

Chapter 13
Women are the Problem

Following the discharge of his appointment to teach the Olympians of the portal and passages to Tartarus, Uriel set out to return to his station outside of the Garden which is in Eden.

Another Seraph fulfilled the work when Uriel was about other work for the Lord, attending to his star, or taking respite. Between the two angels, the way to the forbidden grove was impassable, and never again breached by the questing, the curious, or the ambitious.

The Cave of Treasures was not far, and Uriel desired to see Eve, knowing she was overwhelmed, seeing the world she had wrought. A world of rapidly advancing inventions, medicine, sciences, and art. But also a world of avarice, hubris, imitation, and creeping corruption.

Creation's first five hundred years, a quiet and simple time, was the real forgotten golden age, not the old whispers and dreams of Atlantis that followed. During those early centuries, men remembered God and loved their families and neighbors, hunting, gathering and enjoying perfect weather, fishing, planting, working hard alongside joyful recreation and play.

Adam's sin brought separation from God and eventually physical death, but Eve's anger, vengeance, and gullibility brought the ultimate end of the Age, and the world that was. For she invited the Watchers to help her rid the earth of one monster, and in so doing created ten thousand more.

And still, none of these could match the cunning, intelligence, skill, and life spark of the Screech Owl, Lilith.

Malice brings amnesia, and Eve had wholly forgotten that it was her granddaughter she hunted and hated, that it was the verve of Luluwa, the first princess, which lived on in Lilith. Luluwa, not Azazel, made Lilith invincible. The mother had passed on the fire, the father the brawn and skill. But the latter is only animated and put to use by the former.

Uriel, full of wisdom and discernment, comprehended all of these things, and moreover, how Eve must feel with the weight of it all. Seeing her world usurped by winged things and one-eyed brutes and shimmering spectacles four times the height of a man, coupled with young boys disappearing in the night and rumors, *always rumors*, of a she-devil invading the dreams of the innocent, the first queen was ever burdened, ever distressed, often sad, with a busy mind now trying to stamp out thirty thousand ants with one set of hands.

She would benefit happily from a visit, the angel reckoned.

For Uriel himself personally had held Adam and Eve as they wept grievously outside the Garden that was their home, and the City of God that was their kingdom. Encouraging those to wait for God's timing when their grief and guilt allows them to only operate in the world of the 'now' makes consolation vain. Again and again Uriel had promised the haggard sinners that the Lord would save them, and restore them in the fullness of time.

Following her encounter with Zeus, Eve needs a hug and a cup of tea, not theology today. And he would find her and deliver the same.

***

Over the span of their long lives, the Lord blessed Adam and Eve with over fifty sets of twins for to people the earth. And though each child was a treasure, a gift from God, and of equal value, there was *just something different* about Luluwa that caused her to stand apart from her siblings.

None were like her; nor could they be, for she was the first daughter of Eve. She and Cain were closest to the fount of perfection, suffering none of the disease, defects, or maladies that come with reproduction and recycling of corrupt material in the blood. She was healthier, stronger, and of brighter disposition than her fellows.

And she and Cain, the oldest siblings of humanity, prove that, though predisposed to rebellion and error, the individual is free and accountable: Luluwa choosing good and virtue, Cain choosing selfishness and evil.

The dichotomy continued with the second set of children. For Abel, like Luluwa, was full of faith, verve, mercy, and temperance, but his sister would be the female form of Cain, whom she married.

Awan...

Eve's second daughter's appearance was identical to her own; in hair color, texture and wave, in the eyes, height, visage, and form, Awan was the image of Eve.

But she was naughty. She was selfish. She hurt people for advantage. Her power and presence were equal to Luluwa but she used it for ill, rarely for good.

A perfect mate for Cain, when banished, marked and made to wander east into the land of Nod, she spent several hundred years peopling and founding small towns in what would be called after the Flood (and after the Days of Peleg, when God dramatically carved up the earth that another World Government might not easily be formed, and that liberty might have hope by reason of separation and boundaries), *the Middle East.* With the help of the Watchers, the little towns, tents and villas gave way to the first city, which was named Enoch after the son of Cain and Awan.

For centuries the Queen of Nod relished in her power, persuasion, and position, enjoying a time of doing terrible things with her husband. But in these situations the husband often does not just terrible things (swindling in business, cheating at the market, creating relationship strife amongst friends to gain attention and advantage), but dark things.

Cain was a dark man.

Awan happened upon her husband engaged in congress with the female offspring of a Watcher, a creature who was as much fish as woman. The look upon Cain's face, reveling in the twisted debauchery of it, doing it with religious and ceremonial fervor just to mock the God he had forgotten existed, impacted Awan with burning within her bosom and righteous anger (for adultery is adultery, whether with woman, or angel, or animal, or some devilish combination of the three). She had been Cain's faithful partner when they were but vagabonds with nothing to eat but roots and insects; ever by his side, she stood with the First Murderer. For better or for ill, when starving and when fat, she was the rock that had empowered the crude villain to ascend from pariah to conqueror.

And *now* he would go in unto another *woman*?

And his eyes during the deed!

He loved evil. He relished rebellion. He lusted after lust. And any love he exhibited towards his partner was feigned. The ritual intercourse showed the second princess that true evil can never really have a spouse. For true evil is, in the end, the love of Self above all else. Thus, true evil always dies alone.

Awan possessed the capacity for conviction, and for change. Sorrowful repentance struck her as lightning and she longed for her childhood home, for the innocence of youth, for her father, but above all, for her mum.

At that very moment, Lucifer, unseen, whispered in the ear of the princess: "To thy mother hasten; today, you must go today."

Awan, hearing the voice – subtle, internal, in her head and yet outside her head, imagined but so very real – muddled and mixed its thoughts with her thoughts. She muttered, "I must hasten to my mother. Now. Today!"

The prodigal daughter fled from the land of Nod, praying, crying and singing as she went, for Awan was repentance personified.

***

And Uriel was the Angel of Repentance.

***

Thus did the Seraph and the wife of history's first murderer converge on the First Mother, visiting the troubled lady on the very same day, their arrival at the entrance of the cave just moments apart.

Eve embraced Awan with a melting embrace and a flood of happy tears.

Judgement, none.
Inquisitions and accusations, zero.
Conditions and demands of penance, absent.
Only love.
Only welcome.
Only forgiveness.
Only grace.

This is the way of mothers, and the First Mother was the best mother.

Eve was over one hundred and thirty years older than Awan, but only a few strands of gray hair separated them (and Eve's aging was wrought by long centuries of distress and malaise more than by declining years). They were as twins. Uriel from a field's length off was blessed to observe *two Eves* in a reconciliatory embrace that stopped time and, for a precious moment, seemed to undo the Fall itself.

Happiness filled the air; mother and daughter did not cease to embrace, to cry, to laugh, and to instantly speak of everything and nothing at once. This would have continued into the night, but Eve caught glimpse of the handsome guardian, now clothed as a man, far off.

"Blessed reunion of reunions!" she cried, running to Uriel, beaming with a mother's pride, brimming with the same excitement with which a new mother elevates a newborn before all, presenting her everything to gathered friends and the world.

"The daughter of Eve, I am privileged to meet you and to witness this moment." Uriel's smile when in the guise of a man was much more comely than his fixed and curvy grin when donning his natural face of a serpent.

"Nay, I am the mother of Awan." Eve gave lighthearted correction, elevating the princess above the queen-mother.

That Awan had recovered herself from the snare of wickedness, that she possessed innate regal qualities, confidence and grace like unto her mother, the way she carried herself in contemplative sorrow and was in earnest Eve in every particular, reached into Uriel's heart and possessed it.

The faithful soldier of God had never considered the concept of romantic love, only the service of doing good for good's sake. But in that moment, Uriel realized he had not known that, from the first time she fell at his feet and he had stooped to take her hand in the Garden so many centuries ago… Uriel had been in love with Eve.

Permitting no dishonor to her, neither to Adam, that love was transferred in every part to her shining likeness and express image of her person. Uriel was now in love with Awan.

Rebellion is as witchcraft. It is seductive; it ebbs and crashes like a wave building momentum, then pretends to dissipate, only in due time to return again.

The Watcher Uriel had no part of Azazel's pact, and before the pact, and the subsequent act, had no mind to even look upon women that way. But sin shines a deceptive light of awareness. And temptation is enlightening. Because his peers had done it, he was aware of it, and aware, opened himself to it, and the thinnest breach of interest, as one thread of a tunic once pulled, unraveled dramatically with no hope of re-raveling.

The Most High God dwelt above the firmament; the earth was His footstool and men were as grasshoppers below. All-seeing He would see, all-knowing He would discover, but what is the folly of one grasshopper?

Love justifies and brings turmoil and exponents of problems. That curious creature that is Woman did cause the Angel of Repentance (and repentance means *to change one's mind*) to swerve from his course in service of the purpose of his Creator, and to partake in the very act that had undone the world that was.

Discreetly, in secret, and far away from the intuition of her mother and his dear friend did Awan and Uriel court. Awan did requite to Uriel and the love was equal, passionate, and sincere.

Though they labored to prevent romantic love from fulfilling its course, they, being in love, were helpless. And the forbidden couple yielded to the forbidden act.

Where Azazel's rape and malice wrought by Luluwa, a direct child of Eve, a Primal Witch, Uriel's gentleness, warmth, and risk of losing all (for this was he who had seen the bowels of Hell firsthand, yet even that could in no wise deter his longings) wrought by Awan, Eve's second daughter, another Primal Witch.

And the babe was a lass.

And the lass came to be called Morgaine.

Chapter 14
Fire and Water

"¹⁸ Hast thou with him spread out the sky, which is strong, and as a molten looking glass?"

Job 37:18

"And though they hide themselves in the top of Carmel, I will search and take them out thence; and though they be hid from my sight in the bottom of the sea, thence will I command the serpent, and he shall bite them:"

Amos 9:3

Uriel's heart was full of love, the rest of him filled with secret humiliation. And fear.

Before Awan's belly could show and proclaim their ungodly union to all, the Watcher devised a strategy to hide her away until the babe was born. So the just servant of God began to do what those snared in trouble do: he told little falsehoods. Maneuvering manipulations.

The first lie was difficult: forced, unnatural, and heavy. It temporarily broke his heart, but in an instant a single kiss or passing glance from Awan mended the matter, allowing him to lie anew. For her. For love. For their unborn child.

The Seraph spent an increasing amount of his days away from his station, and he made lesser angels tend to his star. The famous flaming sword was sheathed more than drawn. His time at tea with the First Family increasingly more, his time fending off curious treasure-hunters less.

During their discourses, the desperate spirit invented various facts and factors about the war between the Titans and the Olympians. Subtly, slowly he posited the idea that Zeus and

Poseidon might benefit from Awan's knowledge of Cain and potential leads to locate Lilith's cage. And of course, Uriel would be her personal protector, never leaving her side, so that mother and father could continue in ease, knowing she was safe.

Eve could see the fondness of Uriel towards her daughter, but confused love with sentiment, reminding herself that he was ever kind and friendly to her as well. She rather enjoyed having Uriel and Awan at tea, on walks, or fishing with Adam. To her, it felt like a welcome and happy interlude ere the next dread disaster dropped (for Eve was accustomed to calamity). She perceived nothing inappropriate brewing, and fully supported the angel, the one emissary from above supporting her in strife with the Screech Owl and her struggle for mankind here below.

The half-truth was that Awan would journey to Poseidon.

The full lie was that she was not going to the towering misty mountains where abided the great temple of the gods for a strategic congress about the whereabouts of a long-lost relic. She was not traveling *up*; rather she was going *down* to the depths of the sea.

The fullest of lies was that she was not visiting Poseidon, soon to return to the mother with whom she had just reconciled. Rather, she was going to live with the Lord of the Sea, and others like him, far away from the surface, the stars, and the Hosts of Heaven, away from home for many moons, or forever. For Uriel's plans and plots only spanned the next small lie, then the next. His near-term objective was to see the baby born discreetly, his long-term strategy clouded by the present dilemma.

***

There is a solid dome that separates the primordial waters below the earth from the waters above the earth.

The substance of the vault that protects men from the rushing waters of the Deep is a semi-transparent crystalline glass that reflects the seven primary colors: red, yellow, blue, orange, green, indigo and violet.

The firmament itself has hues of sapphire. The combination of its coloring and the transparent nature of the glass allows men to see what appears as a blue sky above (peering into the waters above the heaven) and creates a *looking-glass* for the angels to see the doings on earth below.

God Himself looks down from His throne. Not because He needs a means of magnifying the theater below, for He is omniscient and omnipresent; rather He *looks down* for purposes of relating to His creation so that they can apprehend, but never fully comprehend, Him. *A good leader meets people at their level, and not his own.*

The angels, who are stars, were created on the Fourth Day, and were thus not around when God created the firmament. However, being intimately involved in the final touches of the Creation Week, the Holy Ones did learn much of its substance and composition, and God permitted them to obtain great knowledge of how to make similar, smaller structures.

The helmets and headdresses of some of the company of the Lord incorporated this skill, making creative ornate 'domes' for their heads, their art and skill honoring the Most High.

After Mount Hermon, metallurgy and glass-molding crafts, which should have benefited men, were instead used to mock and mimic God, with mystical miniature domes protecting little cities along the ocean floor popping up just off the coasts of the earth.

The Watchers favored:
- High majestic mountains to imitate the City of God.
- Diverse, fertile groves to imitate the Garden of God.
- Stone circles of fire to celebrate their courses in heaven.
- Cities beneath the waters to imitate the construct of the cosmos.

Poseidon, who was revered as Lord of the Sea, had three such subterranean kingdoms where god and monster, along with the occasional mortal, could dwell safely, and breathe air if needed.

The Olympian, having heard Uriel's cause, had great sympathy, himself being a proud and good father and seeing the angel's turmoil in endeavoring to be the same. Cronos, Poseidon's father, had done horrible things to him, and he would be different, and opposite of what he had experienced.

The old Titan was envious of the talents and disposition of his youngest son, who was the fairest of the gods, and second only to Zeus in prominence. Hoping to consume the competition, literally, Cronos had swallowed Poseidon, then just a lad, whole. But the malicious act became a blessing to the Olympian, whose will to live forced his father to vomit him out; within the bowels of the gigantic beast did Poseidon obtain the powers of being able to breathe without air, and survived the watery and acidy murk of Cronos's innards.

Yet the Chief of the Watchers, second only to Azazel the Goat, in abject hypocrisy displayed false outrage and offense that Lilith caused the occasional nightmare.

The experience in Tartarus never left Poseidon, and a fear of eternal torment ever rested upon him, lurking behind every arch, staring at him from every window. A shadow of dread of what might come. As a result, his willingness to help the *new fallen angel* was limited to arranging safe entry into one of the three cities and very infrequent visits and involvements, each of which were characterized by Poseidon *looking up* from the depths of the sea towards heaven, the *shadow* surrounding him and a great unknown judge surely looking down.

***

Awan spent her pregnancy in an enchanted bubble underneath the sea.

Uriel traversed to and from Eden, braiding his patchwork of falsehoods and partial truths, misleading the First Mother, whose suspicion grew daily. For example, Uriel would say: "Awan is enjoying the courts of Poseidon, planning for the future, and promises to be home when her work is complete."

These were elusive, practiced lies, befitting *that other serpent* and contrary to all that Uriel had been prior to his failing the test of woman.

Now he was the beguiling serpent.

But when he would visit his love, as a torch in a dark cavern would the Seraph blaze, the brightness of his happy flames filling the dome. He was the sun of that kingdom, flying in rapid circuits, twirling and swirling as a bird of prey displays aerial boasting, his proud plumage on display, racing across the sky.

His pure, smitten joy left trails of sparky vapors and a theater of illumination that drew dolphins, sharks, great whales, seahorses, and every kind of fish, curious and happy (*for love's flame is infectious and good, causing even fish to smile*) to the outer walls of the dome, peering in to view the spectacle of the fiery serpent dancing for his damsel.

The baby baked in her mother's womb was as a special cake made of the best flour, a liberal amount of sugar, and the finest confections. A cake of passionate, thoughtful, romantic, and protective love.

But Uriel's love could not protect the birthing process itself, neither expand Awan's womb.

There was no predictable pattern or tendency that might have warned the forbidden couple to choose an alternative to natural childbirth (for Uriel was a master of blades and surely could have surgically removed the babe). Some of the offspring of the angels were born in regular and size and proportion, then grew tremendously, quadrupling in size by age four or five. Others expanded randomly in the birth canal. Still others remained small.
These were curses and abominations, after all, regardless of intent or care after their conception.

Awan was slender and tall, her frame like the lethal warrior tribes of legend that followed her. Yet she was not overly muscular and also embodied femininity, being curvy and soft. During the term her showing was modest; just a small, tight belly that sat low, perfectly formed around the unborn baby, the rest of her figure wholly unimpacted by the pregnancy. She looked as she had at twenty, or at two hundred, or past her four hundredth year.

Having done her part to people the young earth for centuries, Awan had been through this many times. Nothing was out of place, nothing felt different, nothing gave the mother-to-be caution or concern.

Awan was well. She was fine. The birth pangs normal. The contractions regular. Her pulse steady. Her breathing intentional, regulated, and controlled.

Awan was composed and together – Uriel as a bundle of sticks cast into the creek. Acting identically to mortal men, the new dad paced nervously and asked too many questions.

Zeus had sent his daughter, the demi-goddess Eileithyia, who first taught women how to be midwives, giving them special knowledge of herbs, of postures, of special breathing techniques, of every small detail of how to care for the mother and babe prior to, during, and after delivery.

Eileithyia was confident that all was going well, *until it wasn't*.

A tiny head began to emerge, crowning. Awan screamed, a permanent grimace-smile, happy and expectant tears streaming down her face. The midwives added a symphony of coos and breathing reminders, alternating with synchronized encouragements of 'Not much longer now!'

The little crown was raven-black, already lush and full.

Then the head expanded, unnaturally, as by some cruel and untimely force, instantly doubling, then tripling in size. The shoulders and torso would surely likewise grow and Awan would be torn asunder, and bleed out.

Her angel looked on, helpless and in despair; he had not protected the daughter of Eve. By acting on his love, the Seraph was a killer and no guardian of the precious woman under his charge.

Cain's wife and Uriel's lover was suffering a savage and grotesque death. The baby girl swelled as a sponge, and her tiny bone structure stretched and lengthened in the twinkling of an eye. Awan was a tall woman, and what presently came out of her was twice her height: a perfect, healthy-looking newborn with no anomalies save her gargantuan size.

Two forbidden lovers looked into each other's dead eyes one final time.

Awan's insides were on her outside and the wounds were so jumbled with organs, bone, unidentifiable tissues and gore that many nurses fled, and several swooned.

Uriel was torn asunder as well, broken-hearted. He also was inside-out. The wings no longer burned with brilliant multi-colored combinations of yellows, of oranges, of greens and blues. The feathers no longer made happy sparks.

Instead, the fiery serpent was cocooned in an ethereal flame of crimson red. And only crimson red. The flames were intensely bright, but only around their origin; Uriel was no longer a lantern for the dome. His torch was stamped out. His brightness smoldered.

Enveloped in the red flame of death, six wings creating a self-contained oven, Uriel was killing himself.

"My love. Cease." A hand plunged bravely through the flame, negotiating plumes and finding a hand to clasp. Awan's desperate move added severe burns that bubbled as hot glue to the mutilation that hollowed her from the ribcage down. The Second Daughter of Eve, a woman who knew evil and mischief but had found repentance and love, who held her angel's hand but could not see his face in the flame, instead beheld the face of her daughter and in that moment, also found God, and redemption.

"Cease," she gasped with final and forced whispers. "Look at her." The burnt fingers yanked and jerked, as women's do when husbands are stubborn, distracted, or not listening. She couldn't tell if he harkened unto her plea, but she hoped that he had. "Look at her. Cease. Uriel, please cease."

Women are often wise while men are ever rash. In the moment of dread, instead of looking to her own grievous condition, she turned herself, and her man, towards their daughter.

Her man, her Seraph, did harken. And did cease. Uriel extinguished himself. Still smoldering, he transformed into the likeness of a mortal, that he might better hold the one he treasured more than the whole of the creation, more than the Creator Himself.

Just as he had transferred the love he had had for Eve unto the daughter of Eve, now likewise from Awan unto the daughter of Awan.

Alone, left mostly in the dark with only sufficient light in the chamber to make out the form and outline of her face, the couple beheld the lass. *Born of the Fire Serpent, born in the depths, born in a cauldron of blood and…*

"Our baby was born in such a wondrous and magical place, love." Awan summonsed her final words. "Can we call her Morrigan?"

And the lass was called Morrigan, which is by interpretation 'Born of the Sea.'

Chapter 15
No Place for Them

A veritable battalion of horned aberrations – four-armed giants and winged men with scorpion tails, led by nine merciless, but disordered, cyclopes – had earned a complete flank around Lilith, trapping her in a cave hewn into the high canyon walls of a valley cut by the Euphrates River, whose wide shores were near the place of the impending battle.

The cave was massive, having a dozen pillars of red stone creating natural archways with high-pitched ceilings that could accommodate a hundred men, *and forty-five monsters*, and seemed created for the direct purpose of conducting a dramatic battle. *Or a slaughter.*

***

Michael the Archangel walked with the Lord in the Third Heaven, which is diverse and has many apartments, chambers, mansions, streets, and galleries. They sauntered contemplatively, neither speaking, in a large rectangular hall with a floor that was one constant slate of pearl. The hall had walls, also made of pearl, but these were not continuous. Instead, the pearls were as bricks, and the inlaid gold, rubies and sapphires as mortar. The grange stretched seemingly forever, and was so long that not even an angel could see the ends thereof.

Wanting to speak, but frozen by reverence and a loss of where to start, Michael, whose appearance was that of an armored man with white wings (he did not possess other guises, looks, or forms), just kept walking. *Walk with the Lord and wait. With regard to this subject, say nothing unless asked. And even at that, say little.*

God put a paternal arm around His commander.

"Ask your question." The Lord wanted to call Michael 'my child' or 'my son', but an endearing term did not fit, as the Captain of the Hosts of Heaven was always on duty, always dressed for battle, never breaking character to relax. "But first—"

"My Lord?"

"Have you not considered the sixty thousand diverse kinds of mushrooms, the ninety thousand species of lilac, the plentitude of earthworms, sunflowers, and diversity of big cats in my broad and wondrous creation?"

"Of course. I study, enjoy, and appreciate all of them!" A hint of bewilderment and offense was found in the most loyal of all angels' tone and upon his face.

"Yet you only ever don one suit of armor? Never a tunic, a trouser, or perhaps a comfortable robe?" God said. Then paused, saying naught more, creating an authoritative, godly silence.

More walking.

Then God broke the silence with His infectious, booming laugh, which caused white dust to jump from the pearly floors and the walls to shift, adding their own squealing laughter by way of creaking, then settling back into form again. Knowing Michael wanted to ask the Lord about an unmentionable subject, He had removed the burden of the yoke, and made the weight of the conversation light.

The archangel was grateful, and reading the moment offered, "I cannot commit to a change of attire, but I promise that when next I am with you this breastplate will be silver, and not bronze."

More pearl dust and wall-squealing.

"Ask your question, my son."

"People have died, though not a great number," Michael started. "When they pass away, the breath of life you give them, and give all of us, returns to you. Their soul goes to Tartarus, where they rest in peaceful slumber, not easily disquieted, until the Day where you will raise them up and give them a new body in the Resurrection."

God nodded, affirming Michael's perfect understanding.

"But these... others... the..." and here did Michael formally name the broadest classification of the offspring resulting from Hermon, "Nephilim." (Which is by interpretation *the Fallen Ones*.) "The eldest of them is special and has slain many of her own kind." Michael was unsure if he should actually acknowledge them by their given names, or if that went too far. "They are even now at the eve of another battle, where she shall vanquish many within a great hollow of red stone. Their assumption is their folly and their lack of strategy their undoing. She will kill them. She will kill all of them, easily." The archangel, a typically well-rounded speaker giving equal parts to logic, reason, emotion, warmth and pitch, spoke in a single key, flat and steady, doing all not to cause God to think that he was lending affection, affirmation, or respect to Lilith.

Michael grappled to find the right words and, after additional forced bumbling, finally in a broken sentence gave a confused statement mixed with *the question*. "My Lord, where will those souls go? There is nowhere in your creation for them. Where – *where will they go?*"

Chapter 16
Stacking Ghosts

The cyclops looks ugly, and is perceived as a hideous, drooling ogre that is all teeth and no brains. A mindless brute singularly focused on mayhem and blood.

But though this description would fit the later generations of giants, 'twas not so for the early Nephilim.

Originating and emerging as a 'race' of beings at approximately the same time as the Olympians (and also the direct offspring of Titans), the cyclopes were exceedingly advanced beings with psychic gifts and superior intelligence. Their thoughts were controlled by an overdeveloped, pinecone-shaped gland located in the back of their brains. This region of their mind was responsible for intuition, sense of self, awareness, instinct, and the rapid acquisition, assimilation, and retention of knowledge and information.

The pinecone-shaped gland sat upon a plane within the brain that extended outward between the eyes, in the center of a man's forehead. This led to a description of those having characteristics of heightened spirituality, extreme quick-wittedness and self-awareness as possessing a 'third eye.'

Far from being dumb animals, the cyclopes had no need for two 'normal eyes,' having only the singular *Third Eye* to govern them. Additionally, the bards and poets record that only Uriel and Azazel constructed better armaments than the cyclopes, who bartered with the gods, their swords and spears yielding them great advantage in every trade.

In appearance they were menacing: bald, some with horns, others irregular stubs of bones within their craniums, hairless, with bulky muscles, trim waists and no body fat, their skin the tone and texture of an eggplant. They looked permanently bruised, veiny and contorted, ever looking to be in miserable pain.

The average cyclops was four-and-six-tenths cubits tall, compared to the three-and-three-fourths cubits of an average man. But some cyclopes were as much as seven cubits, which is the equivalent length of ten shoes lined upon the floor, heel to toe.

Brilliant, psychic, and brawny, these were a suitable foe for Lilith, and the best available Nephilim to lead a troop against her.

***

Amongst Lilith's numerous advantages in combat was her ability to ascend. Though built much like a bird, her motions were as the angels, having no need to gain speed or rely upon certain winds, nor space for wing-flapping, to take flight. She could be in a material disadvantage under the head of an axe in one moment, and three stories above her opponent, giggling, in the next.

The cyclopes neutralized this by placing a line of winged scorpion men, to whom they had taught the operation of a bow and arrow, hovering in place on the river side of the valley, and one thousand mortal bowmen on the plateau high above the ridge on the shoreside. The remainder of the troop of monsters chased her along the river below.

The winged scorpion men, like thousands of other angelic offspring, were lower-functioning, frightening, but in many regards harmless, troubled mistakes that had no idea what they were, why they existed or what function they had in the world. They were easily manipulated; the cyclopes simply needed to offer them simple pleasures and riches, show them where to shoot, and command them thusly.

The flying archers loosed a volley in a high arc, creating a type of 'net of missiles' on one side of Lilith's path to escape, causing her to naturally veer from the river towards the red sandstone plateaus and the metropolis of caverns within them.

The mortal counterparts of the scorpions, who were far greater in number, slung a thousand more metal-tipped death sticks into the heavens, and Lilith – now flying just above the shore, the rushing wind pulling her hair into a perfect set of wind-wrought ponytails, uncovering the beauty of her winged, smiling face – laughed at the net of arrows above and obliged her hunters, braking hard right into the caverns.

This will make a nice place to kill them, keeping the fowls and critters from eating carrion corrupt and vile on the riverbanks. I will do my part to keep our shores and waterways clean for fishing, romance, and recreation. The Screech Owl found some pleasure in the 'battle,' though her spirit was at breaking point with the constant attempts on her life. After painting the caves in the blood of freaks and spectacles, she would find Adam and Eve, and then her father, and end this.

"How many boys can I save from the Council of Nine whilst the world and all its inhabitants try to murder me? They would execute me for the very thing *they do*!" she screamed to no one in particular, her laughter transitioning into adrenaline and anger. She twirled in increasingly tight circles, at last being absorbed as a vanishing shadow into a cavern opening; a smaller one, no larger than the circumference of a wash-basin.

The cyclopes' strategy was sound. By limiting Lilith's range with a natural 'roof' of sorts, they could fight her on the ground, head-on. The caves were open and expansive, but they could be flanked at all major entries, and sufficient light could be cast in to create a natural pitch or field of battle.

But the wisdom and brilliance of the cyclopes was outweighed by naivety and the sin of assumption.

All battles are fought in the day.
She is trapped.
She will be distressed.
She will be hemmed in and, suffocating, make her stand.
Our numbers will overcome her.

Five assumptions can lead to one hundred and forty-five deaths.

She is not trapped. Larger caves ever give way to smaller caves because water, like a cutting instrument, seeks its own level, then expands to escape.

She is not distressed – only vexed at another example of unjust hypocrisy by men and gods… and monsters.

THE MORGAINE CYCLE: GWYLIWR

> She lived for a hundred years in a cage; a cave is as an open mountain-top by comparison. She is not suffocating.
> Their numbers amuse her.

Lilith did the opposite of what the cyclopes would have her do: she did nothing. Hours passed, and the sunlight waned as Lilith 'hid' (waited) deep in the circuitry of the red stone cliff along the Euphrates River.

Monsters, like mortal men, lack patience when they think a fight is soon to be had and, failing to master their impulses and bloodlust, began fighting amongst themselves, abandoning station and becoming drunk on mead, agitated and anxious. The army had brought no means of making fire, having neither oil for lanterns nor simple torches. They had chased the witch along the river from dawn, deployed their 'canopy of arrows' plan, and assumed they would be enjoying celebratory revelry, barrels of mead, tale-bearing, drunkenness, and maidens by eventide.

Caverns possess a spooky, layered, hollow sort of obscurity when night falls. Shades betray depth perception, and the eyes see grays with one blink, purple-blue with the next, then, having nothing left to absorb, adjust to pitch-black nothingness.

Masculine impatience, disorganized strife, and the distress of a plan crumbling gave Lilith the advantage; unseen, she easily navigated, as a snake around the farmer's feet in tall grass, around her would-be attackers. She exited the caves and quietly broke the necks (each time cupping hand over mouth, that the death gurgle might be muzzled) of the Fallen Ones that guarded the plank to her left. Then she attended to her rumpled hair and stretched the kinks in her own neck; left, mockingly, now again to the right, now chin to chest, now chin to the heavens. Ready for another stealthy portion, she likewise neutralized the remaining flank, lining the corpses uniformly and with feminine, delicate grace – as a mother would line cakes to cool next to the oven before tea-time with the neighbors.

Only the assembled giants, each of whom had four arms, cyclopes and sundry unnatural beasts remained where they had packed themselves inside the mouth of the great ridge.

Lilith had reversed position and was outside, in the dark, with little bits of moonlight reflecting in droplets of sweat from the form of the Primal Witch. She was as comely as any woman living in the young earth, right to the point her thigh transitioned to the calf of a… calf.

"Boys…" A short conversation, begun with a girlish giggle. "Which of you is chief?"

Nine eyes whirled about. The cyclopes flooded one another with unspoken, mixed, distressed screams via their mind powers.

The Primal Witch could hear their thoughts and, if she chose, respond in like manner, but she opted for words. "No, boys. Those stones are as pillars and if you dislodge them, you will all be smashed into the very marrow you enjoy upon your toast. And" – she shook her head in the dark, knowing that they couldn't see her but that the folly of the plan nevertheless demanded a good headshaking – "I will duck, dodge, or catch the stones, or make one of them five thousand pebbles. And enjoy skipping them back at you."

The unspoken discourse quieted to only a few faint observations, properly noting, "We must attack; we are going to die anyhow."

Lilith agreed but did not respond, instead asking again, "Who leads this troop? Have you a captain or king?"

"I am Arges. And these are my men," the eldest of the nine responded.

"Arges, the blacksmith. Your fame is known to the four corners."

A pause for dramatic impact, for the witch controlled the situation as does a black widow who toys with her prey; winding it tight, then loosening the bonds, only to spin more, as she either sings or imparts some great lesson ere the bite of death.

"You will live this night, returning in defeat and disgrace. Your heart will ever be irreparably broken at the loss of your brethren, and you will pour that anger and sorrow into the weapons you forge for the gods of today and the heroes of tomorrow. Now, deliver a message to your sender; the very one who named the animals at the foundation of the world has forgotten a basic fact of ornithology."

Lilith's authority over others by use of voice inflection and mood exceeded her invincible skill of battle, and was even more frightening than her head-exploding magick. She could undulate from giggling girl to stoic ice goddess, disarming her hearers greatly, rendering them pliable clay for her control and molding. As her thoughts turned to the First Couple, the minutes of toying with her prey had ended, and the cold words of an angry deity boomed.

"Remind Adam that *owls can see at night*!"

***

The Screech Owl indeed let – or *made* – Arges escape; the noble older brother had wanted to die with his kin.

She attended to exactly two scrapes on her left forearm and a minor complaint in her right shoulder. The Euphrates cooled her face and helped clean her hands, discolored and bruised for the short melee.

The dead were left where they had fallen, most of them dismembered in accordance with Lilith's preference to tear away a wing, or an arm at the shoulder, and then display it to her victim as they bled out. Bored, she had taken others at the throat with the snow-white razors in her mouth.

Pausing and breathing for perhaps the first time, she studied the dead.

Like unto a crab, a Nephilim has an outside self and an inside self. Their abominable hybrid bodies, or outsides, housed an identical form that was made of an ethereal substance not fully spirit and as flesh yet not as flesh. A green outline formed around the stacks of 'deceased' creatures.

The Primal Witch could not find an expression or phrase to describe what she saw, thus she coined one. *"These are Otherworldly Beings."* The ghosts of the cyclopes and giants seemed to sleep restlessly, hovering over their outer hosts.

Lilith left the field of battle concerned that her victory had been in vain, or had even multiplied her (and the world's) tribulations. Rather than fighting, the Screech Owl reckoned that she should have made a dazzling escape and fled. Even now, her only thoughts fixed on fleeing to her favorite marshes, high mountains or forest founts, and where to dwell away from all of the madness… alone.

Chapter 17
Britain Before the Flood

The City of God has twelve foundation stones made of every precious gem, with high ramparts of a gold so pure that its walls are as clear, yellow-hued glass. Before Adam's transgression, God dwelt upon the Earth, and His city, after which all holy mountains are but shadows and types, was the center of the world.

The city walls spanned twelve thousand stadia, which is fourteen hundred miles, and no edifice erected by Man or angel has since matched the size, scope, or magnificence of it, in the world that was, neither the world to come. *And God promises to return His city, descending and adorned as a glorious bride, to the place where men rule, in the Ages to Come.*

A direct line from the fixed star Polaris rested upon the pinnacle of the tabernacle within the city, and as direction is concerned, the City of God represented *true north*. For this reason, after the Great Flood would all travelers, regardless of their point of origin, describe Jerusalem as *north*, saying *we must go up to Jerusalem to visit the king.*

If the same visitor stood at the Temple Mount (or prior to and after the temple, the place thereof), facing its gates, then 'north' would be beyond Jerusalem, in a straight line to edge of the world; likewise northwest, northeast, south, east, and west were similarly measured and reckoned. For the world is a mountainous disc, and north is south and south is north, depending upon the perspective of he who holds the map.

And the place where the famed Isles of Brutus reside is to the north and west of Jerusalem, being the *top center* in the sides of the north of the world that was.

Prior to the Great Flood, 'Britain' was still very much part of the continuous land mass and no island at all; neither its daughter islets, nor the Emerald Isle.

From the beginning it was a place of splendor and forests and waterfalls. And it was uninhabited, save by bears and stags and not a few dragons. These were the kings and princes of Britain, in the western world, at the edge of creation.

***

Through an oceanic highway of crystalline tunnels crafted of the same material as the firmament above did Eileithyia, nurse and daughter of Poseidon, hasten the Fiery Serpent with his newborn daughter to exile, far from the wars of gods and men, *and the wrath of Eve*. They surfaced through a brackish body of water at the base of a mountain later called Craig Y Llyn; the sacred pool whence they emerged was ***Llyn Fawr.***

The gray mists of midnight hid the stars, and it would have been impossible to see but for the unsheathed weapon of the angel, whose flaming sword was their torch. It emerged first from the lake, ascending slowly and majestically, casting its illumination round about the entire body of still water.

Curious bears hastened to the shores at the spectacle of light, greeting the first to touch the soils of Britain: a swaddled infant who shivered and shook, but whose eyes, large, bronze, and speckled as a great Persian cat, beheld the bears with equal curiosity. And there was no fear in them, for the Morrigan was in her isle before it was an isle.

The Raven was home.

Chapter 18
Go to Her

Fathers know things too...

Observing Uriel looking upon Awan, Adam saw himself. For he had looked upon Eve with the same fervent and unrelenting, unconditional love every day for over six hundred years.

More than this, he noted the way that his daughter's gaze was reciprocated unto Uriel, which caused the Fire Serpent to burn with more illumination and happy brightness than that of ten thousand suns. The returned, equal love from a woman empowers men, motivates men, drives men to be better men, for God Himself has designed it so. Men are to lead, to provide, and to protect. They are directly accountable to God, and to their wives and children. Women, with their intuition, talent, and predisposition for order, nurture, and creativity, are to help men achieve the same. When in balance and symbiosis, such a union is glorious, the envy of the world – for few find it.

Adam had failed at the tree, not discerning that his partner was bewitched, placing passion and a desire to please her over judgement. From that time, a curse had indwelt both Adam and Eve; men would be given to overbearing tyranny instead of purposeful, just leadership, while women would, by nature, want to usurp the role of their husbands. The divine unity, balance and collaboration was disrupted and ruined. God had withdrawn Himself, leaving the couple who thought they knew better than God to have a go at being God.

And when persons, creatures or things that are not God pretend to be God, the outcome is devastation, calamity, and death. The great misery of the life of Adam is that he instantly understood these things, being of strong conviction and godly sorrow for his transgression, but could not undo them.

He had tasted true, perfect oneness with God, being part of a blessed triangle. After his fall, he carried an accountable, heavy, hyper-self-awareness, the rudder of his conscience steering him away when too domineering, selfish, or failing to listen to his spouse. The knowledge of his own nature and mortality, which unfortunately he would pass on to all of his offspring – *for the life is in the blood, and the blood passes through the man; father to son, father to son, forever* – caused Adam to be an amazingly wonderful husband.

But no scenario or life lesson could prepare him for dealing with a daughter who had fallen in love, and apparently exiled herself, with an angel. And not just an angel, but the very angel who had been in the direct company of his family for hundreds of years. Uriel had been an extended part of Adam's family, the guardian who kept them from paradise but did so with compassion and grace.

Now, it would appear that Uriel had likewise failed his own test. Adam gave passing thought to what manner of expulsion from Uriel's paradise might he suffer. But fathers focus their mind and attention on the safety and happiness of their daughters, deferring their wrath for the boy who wronged them until after their precious treasure is returned, once more behind the shield of a father's love and protection.

The First Man could not directly protect Awan, for she was far away. But his wife was near, and she was broken.

His spouse was a firebrand with an outgoing, relentless disposition. She loved hard and hated harder. Opposite and complementary, Adam was quiet, possessing a great strength of presence and authority accompanied by few words. When he did speak, his message was strategically placed, succinct, usually containing some short proverb, prophecy, or riddle, like a sage or primal druid.

"We cannot hate whom our daughter loves," he said, closely embracing a weeping wife who had suffered the disappearance of her daughter for nine painful months. Her anger was as a full winepress at the harvest. One more drop, just one more grape, and the whole of the barrel would spill in red judgement about the hall. "We don't have to love him, but we have to be loving to him. And abide him," Adam finished.

Holding her close, feeling her protest-filled acknowledgment, he said little else, letting the truth do its own work in heavy silence. *And fearing what God Himself might do unto Uriel.*

Following a forever wait, he at last asked, "My love, will you not reconsider? Empty thy satchel and pursue them not. They will return. I promise. They will return."

Eve wanted to sprint as a gazelle to the peak of Olympus (*if Awan was really there at all*), smite Uriel upon the jaw, catch her lass by the ear, and drag her back to the Cave of Treasures, there to resume tea and gathering herbs and spending their days in jolly jest about the folly of men. *And plotting how to kill Lilith, for Awan was well-traveled and knew the good and the evils of the present world, making her an indispensable ally in ridding the young earth of its she-devil destroyer.* But as her husband held her, Eve realized the vanity of her plan; the vanity of forcing one to 'un-love,' or to be apart from their love. Had not Eve spent every day of her life near her man, her mate? Parenting and emotion often bring great temptation for hypocrisy. Eve considered the counsel of her quiet husband and cried. And considered more, and cried more.

"Yes, Bear," she responded, putting her things away. "To the borders of our old garden I must… just a walk."

The wise husband loosened his embrace, knowing that an upset wife requires two things: *being alone*, and *never being left alone.*

Smiling internally, knowing that women are an impossible mystery made to be loved, not understood, he said, "I will be here if you need me."

She could not muster a smile, but her face acknowledged his care. She took up a walking staff and departed from the cave, alone.

***

Eve spent many hours walking in Eden's easternmost woodlands, wandering without noticing her course, lost in sorrow and contemplation.

Dusk gave way to night, and the Mother of all the Living was without fire, in the dark, and alone.

***

The Screech Owl is stealth.
   The Screech Owl is the night.
   The Screech Owl sees all.
   The Screech Owl is silent.
   She will not be seen unless she wants to be seen.
   And if seen, death is nigh.
   The Screech Owl is *the Huntress.*

***

Aided only by a long, worn, and splintered rowan walking staff, Eve calmly thrashed, clacked and tripped her way to a clearing amongst towering oak trees that were as old as the creation. Perpetually and perfectly drinking of the mist that hydrated the world, the trees were lush, healthy, and thrice times taller than their progeny on Abraham's side of the Great Flood.

The small opening amongst the green giants was all Lilith needed. She had been circling above the tops of the natural towers; the sprawling green tents that were their branches and leaves made a 'swoop and snatch' problematic.

But the prey strolled into an easy kill area.

Eve could not see the Huntress, but she sensed danger, certain that she was no longer alone.

Looking down in the dark to her only ally, an elderly dry stick, she jested aloud, "Where is my angel to light the way home?" She giggled. "Lighting and warming the way for my daughter in his bedchamber, no doubt! Snakes cannot be good at kissing!" Eve's joke was betrayed by broken words and interruptive breaths. She was scared, her humorous monologue into utter darkness notwithstanding.

Lilith stood behind her oppressor: the jealous author of a life of misery, rejection, unwarranted fear, rape and persecution. Matching Eve's step with her step, mirroring her grandmother's every motion and breath as Eve's true shadow.

Eve, overtaken by the matter of her runaway daughter and the fact that she hadn't received one whisper of tidings from the Olympians in nine months, nor seen any evidence that the war with the Titans had in earnest begun, gave no consideration to the idea that Lilith might one night come for her and send her to Tartarus. Rather, she assumed that she was being stalked by some manner of big cat; a jaguar or panther, perhaps.

"My husband gave you your swift and powerful name, Jaguar! You will not eat your mother! Will you?" The monologue of frightened jest continued. *My husband… May he hasten to find me!*

After unreasonable hours had passed, Adam had indeed begun to worry and launched out to find her. Not needing a fire serpent as his lantern, Adam possessed a torch, water, and a spear. But he was above thirty minutes away, searching in the opposite direction of Eve's course.

Lilith did not need thirty minutes, or three. Would she that Eve should fall, three seconds would suffice to finish the matter.

Yet three seconds of pleasure would not undo twice three hundred years.

Hesitation. Conscience.

The Primal Witch had been stayed by these enemies of action before. She had once beheld an innocent child nominated to be her first kill, the forerunner of a swift and great purge that might prevent The Prophecy of the Seed of the Woman. There he had been, helpless and without motion in the very clutches of death, yet unhand him she could not. And would not. The memory of that moment numbed her head and sent a dizzying rush into the tips of her fingers, causing her to twitch, and to pause. And in that pause make a misstep, and in that misstep a twig did snap beneath her hoof.

Hearing this, Eve screamed at the unidentified, invisible thing and fled the open pitch, racing back into the thicket. Back under the oaks.

I see you flee, and fear consumes thee, Grandmother. But alas…

I do not kill children.
I do not kill women.
I kill in the defense of my own beating heart, and I kill bad men.

Lilith watched Eve run through, around, and into the trees, a proud and stately leader under the control of terror in the dark.

I am the dark. I see you as it were noon, though midnight is behind us and the darkness is full.

To save Eve from suffering serious harm, and to exercise centuries of frustration, Lilith cleared the forest with a bloodcurdling, lasting howl. No bear, wolf, or jaguar would approach for fear of the alpha huntress. This helped Eve in the near-term, with the secondary purpose being that Adam surely heard the bellow and could use its origin to find his mate.

Mercy was victorious, but abhorrence remained. She who stalked prey she could not kill yet hated her grandmother, comforting herself by whispering, *"Find another way, find another way."*

Hesitation. Conscience. Fear.

Beyond not being the killer that the whole of the world would have her be, there was another reason, a greater reason, that Lilith would not strike down the woman who had eaten the fruit, whose husband had brought death to all.

Fear.

God had promised to redeem Man by the seed of this woman. As with so many times afore, Lilith heeded God's prophecy, whether she understood it or not. In a world where angels were worshipped as gods and temples erected to creatures that looked like fish, or lizards, or phalluses, the estranged Bride of Satan remembered and feared the real God, full of grace but also justice, who was surely waxing wrathful in His throne.

Lilith glanced towards Polaris, then made intentional effort to put the author of her conviction out of mind.

Awhile I shall stay, perhaps to discover the best way to vex her…

***

"Bear, what was that?" Reunion. Trembling. Trembling in concert.

"No beast of the field nor fowl of the air…" Adam searched for descriptive metaphors in the stead of saying 'devil owl' or 'first witch' but refrained, instead choosing: "It was not of nature. Let us make haste."

The First Couple navigated the wood under the halo of light provided by Adam's torch and the fear that hastened their steps. And their new 'angel' observed as she could, gliding and spying above the oak.

Cut and pricked by thorn and thistle, at last they reached the Cave of Treasures. Empty and exhausted, they collapsed into one another's arms, giving way to deep sleep.

***

"Methinks your night was filled with unwanted tribulation."

"Aye. And methinks the coming tidings will make this morning make last night a light thing and a hundred tomorrows as a sunless sea of black despair."

Fathers know things.

First, Uriel had not woken Eve, choosing instead to allow Adam, whom he knew would rise first, to initiate a whispery dialogue. This was not Uriel's custom. Were the news not dread, he would have awakened Eve with warmth, embrace, or jest.

Second, Uriel's disposition betrayed him ere he spake. He tried for a moment in his serpentine guise, which fared no better than the pained and revealing visage of Man… of a man who grieved.

Lastly, Adam knew the truth for the simple fact that he had seen how she loved him, how she was ever by the angel's side. She was not there, because she was not *here*.

"She is dead," Adam stated. For fathers know things.

Although the present Age had inverted itself and the Hosts of Heaven ruled over men, both beings present, both who had walked with the Lord, knew that the order of creation would in Ages to Come be made aright and that the ministering spirits were indeed under the authority of men, one of whom was Adam, who was made in the image of Most High God.

In the full awareness of this authority did Adam, the quiet, reserved bear, now direct the Seraph. "We will conceal nothing from your great friend and my wife. You will tell us all and straightaway, we will go to her. And you will guide us."

And Lilith the Screech Owl, careful to avoid the new company, did privily hear all…

Chapter 19
Become Their Accusation

Round the fire, in the market, and especially and consistently as part of the nightly sleep-time ritual, Lilith was nightly defamed and accused the world over thusly: *She bewitches parents with nightmares and then, leaving them distracted and terrorized, flies off with their babies, whether yet in swaddling or up to toddlers of five years old. And the children are later found killed in patternistic fashion, having suffered immeasurable cruelty, else never found at all.*

That one hundred newborns had been abducted and murdered in the days before Mount Hermon was true, for Lucifer himself had conducted a plot against humanity, hoping to unleash his weapon-wife on Eve, her children, and the prophesied coming savior of mankind. But evil men donning robes and religious objects did these things, not she.

The plot had failed because Lilith refused to acquiesce to evil, to be complicit in malice, or to be the principal cause of the eschaton. Satan's furious revenge was to defame the first Nephilim – to make her a symbol of evil, a mark, and a curse word for all time.

And in infamy, to be alone.

The lonely owl followed the triad of sad travelers on their long and morose journey from the Cave of Treasures, which is on the outskirts of where the City of God was, to the end of the earth: the sides of the north surrounded by heavy foam and emerald greens, dolphins and every type of sea creature frolicking in the bodies of waters between habitable land and the great ice wall that runs the circumference of the earth. And just before that, the land of bears, daffodils, and dragons.

She observed.

They cried – but were not alone.

They quarreled and judged one another, gnashing and biting each other with grief-stricken hypocrisy. But they did so as a family.

They yelled, but were not alone.

Uriel apologized for all, save being in love with Awan, for he could not deny this truth, neither be ashamed of it. He was able to experience not being alone. But overwhelmed liars continue to lie, increasing their manifold problems. He did not disclose the manner of her passing, saying only that she had died at the hands of a Watcher.

Eve did not easily nor soon forgive Uriel, whose increasingly egregious lies stacked to the tenth heaven. How could her warden partake of forbidden fruit and the Creator do naught, whilst she was cursed to experience his wrath's reminder every month, suffer the pains of birth-giving, have her nature changed for the worse, and be forbidden from tending HER sacred grove and garden?

Eve verbally scourged her angel. He tried to respond, rationalizing, justifying, shaming himself and his glorious pedigree as one of God's very elect. Adam the Wise tried to be the peacemaker, mediating the hot heads of two leaders.

All were fractured. Together.

They cursed the gods – together.

They combatted feelings of losing faith – as a family.

They doubted everything; they bemoaned everything. They were a miserable troop, having lost a daughter so recently reclaimed, and a forbidden lover stolen so soon. A triad of wailing, brokenness.

But a broken triad is preferred to a solitary vagabond.

Observing these things, Lilith, whose spying gave her centuries' worth of family secrets by reason of the constant argumentative, grief-borne wailings, started to consider that she might let them alone. *They have ruined themselves. Leave them to the misery of a future under the thumb of Cronos, or as subjects in Poseidon's benevolent dictatorship in Atlantis. The best way to defeat Man is to leave him to his own folly. They have nothing.*

But they did not have nothing.

Uriel was not conducting the troop to the body of Awan that her parents might behold her, kiss her forehead, and say a final goodbye. The princess was buried deep within the sea, for the gore of her passing allowed for no viewing by grieving parents.

Rather to the daughter of Awan, the baby Morgaine, did Uriel conduct them.

"One final untruth have I spoken." The seraph's hue buzzed, glowing with blues and yellows, framed by thick gray smoke that outlined his form as he flapped. His great wingspan blocked the entrance to a small stone cell: a wee domicile hewn into the side of a gray, stony mountain, the side of which was splotched by bright green moss, garnished with every kind of flowering vine.

The home was luxurious and no crude cave. The door was wooden and covered in ox hide, its frame crafted from three perfectly smoothed blue stones. The sweet aroma of soup and the crackle of flame indicated that a hearth provided heat and light to the comfortable forest cottage.

And the First Nursemaid and a very large and thriving baby reposed within.

"Does my Awan lie within this marvelous cave?" Eve ignored Uriel's comment, marveling at the simple beauty of the enchanted place on one hand, and having reached her limitations in suffering his dishonesty on the other.

"She does not, for Awan rests not here—"

"Ah, this is a place of rest then, and a peculiar and delightful place it is." Eve attempted to peer around his wings, her hands fanning fruitlessly to clear the smoke and improve her view of the cottage. "How long shall our respite continue, and when shall we continue on to my daughter?" Impatient, she tried to proceed around, or if necessary through, him.

Perceiving that her purpose was singular and that she would barge through the door ere hearing his final confession, the Fire Serpent unsheathed his sword and ignited it. It whirled and sizzled with the righteousness that he had lost; the blade was full of power and authority, the fallen wielder having neither of these.

Blue and yellow were replaced by red. Great pupils of single slits gave dread glare. Fearsome, terrible and glorious.

The Guardian of Eden would be heard, even if it meant using the gross hypocrisy of taking arms and posturing once more in the fullness of his former self. A fearsome, whirling fire-sword brandished by a flying, livid snake would fix the audience's eyes, and ears, upon him.

"A Watcher slayed the damsel Luluwa," he began.

Lilith the spy privily heard this. A rush of rage overtook her, her mind returning to the cave, to the birdcage, to the infanticide, to Azazel, her father, and to Satan, her husband.

"And likewise, a Watcher slayed the fair damsel Awan," Uriel continued.

Hearing this from above – for the Owl is the Huntress, and can hear, unseen by her prey, from great distance – Lilith did screech, cursing her father aloud, assuming that the lust-addled rapist had again indulged his insatiable desire to have, to consume, and to hurt.

Uriel, hearing the far-off cry, interrupted his confession. "Grave danger circles above—"

But Eve suffered not the parenthetical moment. "At the tip of your sword you have placed your friends, your family, only to stop the melodramatic spectacle to warn of eagles and sparrows? Foul spirit!" An angry mother can walk through a sword, and the bears that protect their cubs from their maniacal fathers were first referred to as *Evecubs,* after the protective ferocity of Eve. The first mother bear was not to be detained; she *would* see who or what dwelt beyond the threshold of the delightful stone cottage cut into the gray mountains in this marvelous retreat at the end of the world.

The Fire Serpent returned to form, dismissing what lurked above. "What Azazel wrought by malice and abuse, I have wrought by love—"

A baby! A child is kept behind the muttering flap of that pitiful worm. Hence the cozy abode, hence the inviting precipice, hence the remote location in the northmost recesses of paradise. HIS DAUGHTER IS IN THERE! Lilith undulated between intrigue, nostalgic disgust, and hot anger.

Instantly her strategy was formed.

AND HER GRANDDAUGHTER BESIDES. Thousands of accusations of abduction and the robbing of infants. How many times has Grandmother personally and falsely accused me? The burning of my dwellings, the superstitious talismans that young sons wear in the field, cursing and shaming me. The smirk of vile priests doing that which they do with impunity, knowing the charge will be laid upon my head. Eve did this, Eve – the source of my pain, the instigator of my suffering. Lilith in flight, her back to the sky, inverted herself and flew as one glides in a pool, floating on her back, wings at her side making slow, deliberate flaps so that she sailed as an arrow. She looked towards and beyond the sun. *Whatever the cause, I cannot kill her, but I can become their accusation, stealing her last chance for joy – murdering her peace, at least, in too long a life.*

The sailing arrow stopped instantly, spiraled thrice, and descended to the location of the quarreling trio outside the cozy cottage, set serenely in a wood, near a waterfall, within the womb of one of Pre-Britain's lovely and hollow hills.

***

"Aw. How… romantic." The Primal Witch, too swift to hedge, touched down between the winged serpent and the door. "I wonder if our kinswoman looks like me."

Lilith smiled, whispering words that brought dark clouds (rain did not exist in this Age, and dark magick served as proxy for water: a swirl of dark blue fear, a canopy of malice and cold revenge) o'er the scene, shrouding the cottage, and the visitors, in darkness.

The angelic wick flared as a new candle, crackling in declaration of itself, then burgeoning into full flame. Likewise did the sword of Uriel slash down to his right, then again across the air at the level of his waist, the swings and swoops of a knight that precede a mortal duel.

The happy she-devil fanged herself by reason of her grin, for fangs are never suited to smiles. Three little droplets of blood decorated the corners of her mouth, as bright red wax, heated, racing along a porcelain chalice.

The light provided by Uriel enabled Lilith to meet the eyes of her grandparents; first Adam, next Eve. With her mouth, or perhaps her mind, she instructed them: *Run!*

And she was convinced that the Fire Serpent, at the very same moment, beseeched them to do the same.

Chapter 20
Lilith Versus the Archangel Uriel

God's most favored angel – the Guardian of Eden, the Archetype of Hades, the one given keys to the most secret places of Hell, the most highly esteemed of the Holy Ones – now stood toe to toe, *or rather tail's end to hoof,* with the kingdom of Satan's first and greatest abomination, the fanged visage of evil itself. The creature, a tall, slender blend of an owl and a goat or bovine-kind, yet with the form and elegant curves of Luluwa, embodied the sensual appeal of God's most fair creation. Only her eyes were not fair, being wholly red, having neither pupil nor iris.

God's angel: a disgrace, a tangle of dishonesty, hypocrisy, and shame. The Fire Serpent forgetting God and venerating his passions, his desires, and his loins.

Satan's bride: a life of protecting children, punishing the sinister and the cruel, and fearing God.

God's angel had defamed himself; Satan's bride was defamed by gods and men alike. Irony and Paradox were now to join in mortal clash.

In his heavenly form, the Seraph was a winged serpent with a muscular, man-like torso, two arms topped by rounded, marble shoulders, six wings, and no legs. His tail was the length of two men, spined and spiked, more akin to a dragon's than of the snakes that toil about in the weeds.

He would fight her in the dark, giving his own light as an intermittent lantern when needed, hoping that shadow and confusion would allow his long weapon to find its aim. And then, when battered and beaten, the might of his flaming sword would finish the deed, slaying the mighty witch.

Lilith brandished no weapon save the ten razors that were her fingers and thumbs, the fangs that could bite through steel and crush bones, the strength of five thousand oxen, and the speed that made arrows as sloths and lightning as a slow-dripping raindrop upon the bark of a tree.

And magick.

Giggling at his preference for darkness, the Owl abandoned her position near the door and retreated outside the range of Uriel's tail. Then she unleashed her *brain-splatter spell*, the technique favored when the threat was validated, else when she wanted to punish, else when the fight caused the Primal Witch great boredom.

The first part of the spell caused the receiver to see anew in their mind's eye – as if happening in the present, only much more rapidly – every sin and shortcoming ever committed.

Every lie.

Every indiscretion.

Every failure.

Every detailed moment of embarrassment.

And then, whilst the lightning storm in the mind raged, burning every circuit with unbearable pain, and the head could contain no more the weight of the memories, would the brain-pan be breached and the head explode. All of this happened in a matter of seconds that felt as a lifetime to the victim of Lilith's judgement.

But the spell only worked in part on the archangel: the first part.

Her wiles did indeed cause him to see anew his failures, sins, and rebellion. The surge of dark sparks bounced through his head, causing him to fall upon his belly, but not perish.

Pleased with the outcome, and glad there was more punishment to inflict, the Owl mocked the Serpent, "Upon thy belly shalt thou go, and dust shalt thou eat all the days of thy life."

Curious as to why she could not crush the Watcher's brain with her mind, she approached the wounded warrior and stooped to turn him over. As she did so, he found her forearm with his sword, recovered from the hex, and bolted upright, ready to deliver another blow, which she dodged.

Then another – she rolled – then another, and she stepped forward and to his left, inside the kill range and out of danger.

Lilith was, alas, too swift even for a general in God's army. But Uriel did cut her, and she clutched at the wound: a gash that ran the length of her forearm. Most weapons had no effect on the demigoddess, but this wound concerned her. *I don't know if I would become one of those green orbs bobbing around upon the shores of the Euphrates, and I don't want to find out.*

He came again, five thrusts finding air and nothing else. A slash nicking her thigh. An overhand strike that she caught betwixt both hands, clasping just above his upon the hilt.

This caused a clinch between the two combatants, a death stare by two legends, and neither would yield. His godly eyes glared into her devil-eyes, and her red eyes searched the flawed, beautiful being before her.

Lilith was stronger.

Uriel could not hold long. Soon she would earn leverage by reason of a higher position on the sword and push it, and him, down, clinging onto it in vain, at last disarming her opponent. To prevent this, the winged serpent ignited his wings, enveloping both of them in heavenly flames.

The Owl unhanded his weapon and launched herself into the air as though a full-sized flaming arrow whistling in a high arc. The speed of her flight extinguished the flames, and she hastened to stamp out burning spots on her calves and her own wings.

Whilst still in flight, Lilith examined herself. *I am cut, I am burnt, and this fellow hath disheveled my hair!* The originator of the witch's cackle cackled for pleasure. She had never been in real danger, having not yet countered with an offensive of her own. After soaring to a point where she could see that Adam and Eve were well away from the fighting – *I will deal with them next* – she fixed her gaze upon Uriel, who remained illuminated as a welcoming beacon outside the structure.

Uriel did not give chase, fearing that Lilith would use her speed to again earn a position between him and the doorway. Perceiving no other option, he waited, and foolishly absorbed her attack.

Where the swing of his blade missed oft, her hands never did. Uriel cut Lilith once, clipped her once more, two of sixty attempts finding their target. Lilith struck Uriel thirteen times... of thirteen.

Slashes to the face.

Knees to the liver.

Locking maneuvers that dislocated the fingers, the wrists, and the left shoulder.

Uriel made imprecatory prayers above, calling for Michael or Gabriel to come unto him, to fend off the predator, to detain the witch.

But Heaven was silent.

Lilith pinned the snake to the ground, causing him to literally eat dirt, and gathered the starting point of one of the angel's glorious wings in her hand. She yanked violently, cleanly separating it from his body.

Flashing and glowing, vanishing into an invisible realm then back into the prism of the living, detached from consciousness, the torn Seraph settled into a final state, transformed into the likeness of a man. Lilith stood him up slowly, helping him stand that she might behold the brokenness of God's Elect. Battered, bruised; soundly defeated.

Caring not for his own body, Uriel mustered a desperate lunge towards Lilith's feet. Confused, she peered down. *Is he groveling? Praying to me? What is he doing?*

The sword – the Sword of Power. Broken.

What had been one perfect, straight blade now existed in two shards, asymmetrical and ruined. Uriel wept.

Seeing this, the Owl added insult to loss, saying, "I will keep this and gift the smaller fragment to... your child." A satisfied smirk. "My child."

Lilith took Uriel *the man* in her arms in the same manner as she had flown with the innocent lad she'd stolen from his happy slumber, so long ago. To the top of the rocky gray mountain that hosted Morgaine's cell she ascended, finding the right spot to kill the fallen angel.

Finding the same, she laid him upon a flat limestone, a type of naturally occurring altar at the zenith of the mount.

The witch opened her right palm, making straight the five killing instruments, then drew them back as a cobra, coiling and quivering, gathering lethal force, properly building for the death stroke.

"My little white owl."

The voice alone robbed Lilith's lungs of their wind. As she searched for the sound's origin, Uriel rolled from the limestone, crawled to the clifftop, opposite to where the cottage was located, and slid from the mountaintop, bruising face, bashing knee and chest, backside and frontside as he disappeared into a kingdom of crags, caverns, and tunnels below.

Lilith cared not that Uriel had flung himself either to death or hiding. *Do angels die?* She shrugged. *Besides, I can kill him anytime.*

The voice. **That voice.** Her only concern.

"Would you, who fears the Maker of Monkeys, really kill one of His most cherished children? Leave him to me; worse things will I do than even you can imagine."

"No!"

Lilith understood that if Lucifer wanted Uriel alive then God had no part in it, the Deceiver's deceptive words notwithstanding. Liars do not ferment like unto good wine, bettering with age; rather do they rot like sulfur and muck. He could not twist her intent, neither manipulate her to continue his bidding. *But where is he?* Lilith, not finding her husband but now knowing she must finish her task, scurried down the hill. But the manifold caves and small places rendered finding Uriel, or recovering the body, folly.

Another time, Fire Serpent. Lilith, shaken more by the unwanted visitor than by her epic duel with an archangel, composed herself, then returned swiftly to her purpose.

Eve – who, predictably, had discerned Uriel's fall and progressed to the cottage, there to make her stand against Lilith – approached the lavish door, where her husband already stood. As the door was creaked open, Eve cocked her head, trailing its movement, desperate to catch a glimpse of the treasure within. And as she began to see—

Slam!

"Ah, a girl child. So tall!" The Screech Owl now covered a fully *shut* door, spreading her own wings, simulating Uriel's posture of old. "You are used to being banished and shut out, are you not?" she hissed. "You will never see her."

Chapter 21
The Nursemaid

By the reckoning of the bards, a short generation is two score and a long generation three score and ten, or seventy years.

From the Creation to Mount Hermon was seven long generations.

From Mount Hermon to the Olympians was three generations.

From the Olympians to the Great Flood was thirteen generations.

Thus for over one thousand years did the Watchers rule directly over the Earth, taking daughters of men for wives as it pleased them and transforming the world into a realm of giants, monsters, and every manner of curious creature.

In the midst of the thousand years did Lilith defeat Uriel the Archangel in the far north, at the world's end, and banish Adam and Eve from those lands. Seven generations of the Nephilim remained before the world that was met its ending.

And the perversion was just beginning…

At this time did Zeus and a company of heroes overthrow their untoward parents, using the particular iron shackles Uriel had given them to lock the Titans in the prison prepared for them from the foundation of the world: deep beneath the Gates of Hell, at the mouth of the grotto beneath their own sacred mount.

The old gods, bound in darkness with no hope of escape, moaned in terror and despair, daily and nightly. From heaven on earth, where they had enjoyed a boundless supply of temple prostitutes, grapes and fatted calves, to a ceaseless, repetitive torture by the devices designed to visit cruelty upon their ethereal flesh. Heaven on earth… to a literal and real Hell.

The cries of those gods could not be heard by reason of the depths of their prison, but there were stories – whispers and warnings that discouraged immorality and injustice. The fables and reports caused many of the Hosts of Heaven to forsake their earthly families and return to the corridors of heaven, there to cower, sometimes to hide, else to sing hymns of repentance, wailing ballads begging for divine pardon.

The godly man, Jared, begat a son, Enoch, who loved the Lord and walked with Him. This Enoch, though he shared a forename with the son of Cain and Awan, was opposite in character, conduct, and impact on history. Enoch son of Jared built hope; Enoch son of Cain built cities and commerce. Enoch son of Jared traded in joy and encouragement; Enoch son of Cain merchandised in corruption wrought of gold, and power wrought of dark sciences.

God did exalt the second Enoch, who was the seventh from Adam (for Adam begat Seth, who begat Enos, who begat Cannan, who begat Mahaleel, who begat Jared, who begat Enoch), catching him away up into Paradise and giving to him many prophecies about the End of Days.

The Third Heaven became the permanent dwelling place of Enoch, and the Fallen Ones did find him there, pleading with him often that he might beseech the Lord in their stead, desperate for him to be an intercessor for them.

God was yet silent regarding the Hosts of Heaven, except that He appointed new angels to the post and position of Watcher. The Most High's anger surely kindled towards those who mocked the creation with abominable offspring and designs of their own. But, as the twilight of the first day of history drew nigh (for a day is as a thousand years to God), He showed little acknowledgment of the pretenders that governed His earth; rather towards Man, whom God had given agency over the realm, did His judgement kindle.

For was it not men worshipping the creature instead of the Creator, and choosing to give themselves over to uncleanliness and perversion? Was it not the sons of Cain developing sinister religion, devising new ways daily to venerate dark deeds and impose cruelty upon the fatherless and the weak?

Michael and Gabriel, when in the company of the Father, could feel His sore displeasure. They knew fully that the same God of grace and mercy must, by nature, also need be the

God of justice. And justice simmers slowly, until at last it boils over.

They dared not enquire about, neither utter the name of, their kinsman, Uriel.

As for Zeus, he preferred his throne in the clouds, enjoying the eagles, his siblings, and the love of his many wives. But Poseidon loved politics. And the Lord of the Sea became regarded as a sort of High King, ruling through ten governors over a world called Atlantis.

Into this era of antiquity was born the goddess Morrigan, whom the bards of Cymru and Llydaw call Morgaine, ascribing to her the Breton rendering of her name, on account of her long years in her beloved and enchanted forest of Broceliande.

***

"May I hold her?"

"She is too tall to be held." Eileithyia laughed nervously. She, too, was a goddess, but dread and fear had overcome her, so she tried jesting with the dark huntress imposing her menacing presence upon the small room.

It worked.

"I see that." Lilith likewise laughed.

"But you can cuddle her from the side, like this."

Lilith rocked the lass, holding her just as instructed by the babe's mistress, gently burying Morgaine's head in her bosom. The hardened warrior found herself humming gently, making cooing sounds, wearing a full and permanent grin that could not conceal her fangs, maternal tears streaming and streaming.

"What is she called?"

"Morgaine, for her mother spent many days in my father's kingdoms below and favored them greatly above life up here upon the dirt."

"This wondrous place notwithstanding, I agree with her conclusion." The two shared another laugh together – as women, as mothers. Babies bring laughter and giddiness to any abode, and every circumstance.

You are Uriel's fire and Awan's naughty brilliance, and Grandmother's resilience, aren't you? My pa a goat, yours an archangel. My fire princess born from the sea, what greatness you will be!

"I cannot rear my cousin." Lilith returned from baby-induced bliss, and cold pragmatism captured her face and tone. "They will never stop hunting me. Her life would be as a vagabond, filled ever with danger and death. And she might be used as leverage to harm and destroy me. So precious a treasure shall never be used as an instrument of vendetta or politics."

Eileithyia wanted to provide the obvious solution – that Morgaine should simply be returned to her natural grandparents, to whom she belonged. The nurse was brave before Lilith, but not that brave.

"My sentence is this." When Lilith drew authority into her lungs and spoke in this manner, she sounded exactly like Adam. *Few words. Crisp words. Leaving no space for argument.* "You will be as mother to Morgaine. You will reside here, living in this magical little stone cell at the end of the world."

Any person that looked upon, or moreover, stepped within the cottage instantly felt at home, for the place was distinct, warm, *special*. Thus, the nursemaid made no protest at all, seeing herself enjoying the abode and thinking that Morgaine would surely go where she liked, how she liked and with whom she liked within a few short years, being a goddess, anyhow.

Lilith went on: "I saw, in flight, a forest to the south and east of this place. I will make a secret encampment there. I shall visit you and protect her where I can. But sparingly, and not oft. There are evil men in this world, and I cannot be as a recluse, being idle as they harm—" Lilith rocked more, hummed more, cooed again. "The most important person in a girl's life is her father. Having lost hers, is there someone you can charge alliance with you and fulfill that office in baby Morgaine's life?"

"Yes. My father Poseidon will send him."

"Well." Lilith nodded, rising. Then she turned back, adding, "Speaking of fathers: wrap and protect this."

But she kept the smaller shard for herself, and departed.

Chapter 22
The King of the Tylwyth Teg

"You are NOT my father!"

It was Morgaine's favorite, and most oft-used, back-biting excuse when laziness usurped study.

"Not this again." The Puck shook his horned head, frustrated, yet suppressing laughter. "The seven sacred herbs, *daughter*. Single-mindedness now."

The child cursed in the contrived, conjured languages of youth, then yielded. The sooner the answer given, the sooner today's schooling would conclude – the sooner the unrelenting elf (whom she adored) would relent.

"Valerian. Skullcap. Wormwood. Catnip. Vervain. Hypericum. Buckthorn."

"Perfect!" A happy elf. "And the nine secondary herbs?"

"Father!" An unhappy demigoddess. The list was rattled off just the same. "Tell me, elf, why did the One who made the ones who made us create plants with healing properties if Adam and Eve were intended to live forever? Is it not only the sick that require medicine?"

"Why does a seven-year-old burden herself with such weighty, philosophical considerations? Better to enjoy the flora and fauna, the stags and bunnies here at Paradise's edge, aye?"

"You answer in this manner when you don't have the answer, elf." Morgaine was enraptured with herself, having bested her impish paternal figure.

"What know you of *elves*?"

"Nothing save that you are their chief. And that next you will probably bid me classify and name seven kinds of them!"

Her response was one part musing, one part anticipatory regret over more schooling and study sure to come.

"Seven – or seventy, daughter."

"You are not my father!" she raged. Then, when her feigned anger she could no longer contain, the lass squealed in laughter and squeezed him with the whole of her might, nearly killing the Puck by reason of her titan-like strength.

He reciprocated the embrace.

"Your question is excellent, Raven." He looked to the heavens, searching for an answer, as parents do, hoping to provide clear and accurate teaching to his child. "The Creator made everything, and it was good. Disease, death, illness, and misery were not part of His design or purpose. But, as demonstrated by how you like to fish when I prefer to paint, or wear black-dyed skins when others may prefer plaids or red dyes, He gave them free will. Knowing the ending from the beginning, God knew they would rebel, that they would turn from His ways, and that they would ruin His perfect creation."

Pausing for a time so that she could consider these things, he continued. "Thus did He ingrain within creation itself all that Adam and Eve, and their progeny, would ever need to help them endure the consequences of their own choices. They would turn on Him and choose their own end, which is death. But He would provide all provision to lessen the impact of their great folly, allowing for a fulfilling, long life in their broken flesh until the day when He would restore them, and the whole of the creation, with a *new body*."

The girl clipped a small bud of silky purple vervain and looked at it with greatly expanded inspiration. "Because He knew the flesh would become flawed and sickly and potentially experience tumors, the One who made the ones gave us vervain to heal the tumors, ere there were tumors. Thus does the creation itself declare that God has a design and plan for us all!"

"For those whom He made, aye." The elf finished the theology, herbology and philosophy lesson with the admonition: "Just as I request that you be home from your fishing so that we can sup by eventide and, knowing you will disobey and stay out well past the owl's hours, hide salted meats and dried fruits in your scrip. I know you will break our dinner engagement, but that doesn't mean I want you to starve."

Morgaine smiled. "You are a wonderful da."

"I'm NOT your father," the elf reminded her.

***

Alas, he was not the special lass's father, for she was sired by Uriel the Seraph and the second-eldest female of the First Parents. In this regard was Morgaine of the very oldest stock, being the female offspring of a Watcher and a daughter of Adam and Eve. Lilith and Morgaine, though born almost a thousand years apart, shared this lineage, each being so close to the fount of pure blood combined with the mysterious substance of angels.

And the elf, whose name was Gwyn, was likewise of prestigious pedigree.

***

Morgaine forgot nothing, and remembered all.

"The elves, Da. Tell me of the elves."

"From 'why did God contain medicine in plants' to 'what are sprites,' all in one day? Perhaps the mind has had sufficient learning for the day?"

"There is only today. If the mind empties itself anew each morn, then would I have to learn yesterday's lesson afresh, retaining nothing, doomed to dwell in ignorance." Morgaine was most pleased with herself, and took to dancing around him in spirals, basking in her continued intellectual victories.

Knowing there would be neither quarter nor rest until the student's curiosity was quenched, the teacher taught.

"The world is filled with a diversity of every kind of being and, in the process of time, as with the creatures of the world, we who are of the *Otherworld* have class and kind of reason of repetition and breeding. At the start this was not so, for one of the Sky People, whose appearance was like unto a falcon, might get by a daughter of Eve an ox, or horse. For the ingredients of all is in one, and the ingredients of one is in all."

"Is this why two gray wolves sometimes give us a black pup?"

"But only after their own kind – yes!" Gwyn marveled at Morgaine's brilliance. "The compositional contents for *every kind of wolf* is contained in *every kind of wolf*. But over the course of time, certain traits – tail length, paw size, pelt color, and more – reoccur more frequently due to preference of mating, dominant characteristics in the bloodlines, and so on. If the pup with a longer tail is preferred or more desirable in a certain pack, then in the process of time, the pack will become known for long tails. But sometimes – "

"Sometimes a short tail is born amongst them!" Morgaine, aware that she had never seen a mortal, wondered, *Am I a short tail in the pack? Do I belong to a pack at all?*

"Astute!" Gwyn continued. "With our kind, classes, races, and kindreds have emerged and organized themselves. In the broadest sense, an elf, which is also called a faerie, is a being hailing from the female offspring of the Watchers, and the giants from the male.

Most faeries and giants reproduce, but marrying daughters of Eve, else others of their own kinds.

"But sometimes there are divergent permutations and combinations of everything betwixt and between, on account of giants lying with fae, even though the races are, and have been from the start, ferocious rivals."

"Such things would seem to bring about many problems," the philosopher observed.

"Such things should never have been in the first place." Gwyn's expression challenged the lass to deconstruct the situation further.

"None of us should be here," she concluded, her speech plain. "Do the giants have a king?"

"Indeed, the giants bow the knee to Poseidon, likewise the heroes and the mighty men, and moreover most factions of mortals as well."

"But these fae, did not the Sea Lord place a king over them?"

"Indeed he did. A king they have, daughter." The elf aggrandized himself, charmingly – "The best of lords." Then he curtseyed formally, bending at the waist before his foster-child. "A naturally mischievous and naughty lot, they need a leader who is just, fair, strong, of impeccable character and wisdom that surpasses comprehension. But alas, the King of the Faeries is in exile, rearing a Primal Witch."

At last, the teacher had befuddled the student. That one he spoke of so highly must, of course, be himself, and her eyes narrowed, the bewildered seven-year-old demanding, "What is a Primal Witch?"

Chapter 23
God Intervenes
The Shining One and the Hermit

Five hundred years before the Great Flood, at the beginning of the seven generations of antediluvian Nephilim, God peered down to the earth, which is His footstool. The deeds of the Fallen Ones were viewed before the glory of His throne, the dread of His judgement. At last, He intruded upon the plans of the disobedient spirits who had taken the affection of those He loved – those who had corrupted His good and perfect creation.

The Fae King's words to the child Morgaine were true. As the Otherworldly Beings multiplied on the earth (although such designation is not altogether fitting, for only the parents of the Nephilim are from another realm; the abominations themselves are earthly, being formed down below, side by side with the sons and daughters of men), races, factions and bloodlines were arising, and the new generations of the Fallen were different, and increasingly far worse, than their forebearers.

The gods themselves had shifted their view of humanity from something comely, beautiful, and desired, to something to be assimilated, or stamped out.

After all, the gods knew how to govern justly. The gods had no poor – those without fathers or homes were cared for, by policy. The gods used gold as a trustworthy and neutral means of exchange, understanding its intrinsic value. Their economies were fair, without usury, and thriving.

The gods understood the wheel, the pulley, the gear, and forces. They invented flying contraptions and vessels for roving in the deepest seas. The gods gifted this and other knowledge to men, who in turn corrupted and perverted it, showing themselves worse in lust for power and position than any winged visitor from the sky.

And mirroring the pattern of their gods, the sexual immorality and perversion of men bourgeoned in frequency and variety. After all, if an angel could bed a horse, a dolphin, or a damsel, why could not men forsake their women and likewise lie with beasts of the field, and each other?

But unlike their gods, who contained the generative properties of all life in their loins, the men produced no crossbreeds, just disease, debauchery, insanity, and a cliff-like decline of new mortal babies being born.

And men – who are made to be strong and rugged but to use their might for protection, for temperate, soft, and calm decision-making, for the greater good of their homes and communities – instead became violent, impulsive, and weak, as a pebble unchecked becomes a boulder.

God was forsaken almost entirely. The angels were as God and as Men, and the men became as women, and as animals. As goes the man goes the family.

When the family disintegrates, civilization falls.

The hubris of the gods, enraged and impatient in their dealings with men, increased; their advanced civilization began to swoon and creak under its own reaction. Divine liberty and principles of good and glory gave way to rules, controls and vain efforts to tame the enemy of all that is good – namely the flesh of sinful men.

Giants especially increased as a problem as well. Once advanced seers and noble ones, these sort before the Flood thought on nothing else but to devour the flesh of mortals and one another. Cannibals and blood-suckers all, the heroes and demigods conducted countless operations to hunt scores of giants, knowing that if they did not, entire cities would fall to these tower-like locusts.

Men were riotous, giants vampiric, gods organizing into factions.

Some elder Nephilim, who were born directly of the first two hundred Watchers, ensured a linear descent of male demigods that carefully married and got children only by mortal women, else the female offspring of their own kind. Moreover, they possessed knowledge of reproduction and were careful only to marry second (or further removed) cousins. These were healthier, more angelic abominations. Known abroad as the Shining Ones, their traits included luminescent, pale skin, emerald eyes, and wavy, wild hair of orange and bright red.

A closed society, carefully guarded, inaccessible to outsiders. The 'purest' of the monsters. *And the perfect opportunity for the Lord God to move against those who would breed mankind out of existence.*

***

There lived in these days two men, both called Lamech.

One was the son of Mathushael, of the line of Cain; the other the son of Mathuselah, of the line of Seth.

The Lamech of Cain was the first to enter into polygamy, formally having two wives – one to govern hearth and home and to mind the children, one for pleasure alone. This Lamech was a deviant, a disgrace, and a villain. Lamech of Seth, conversely, was a quiet, private man who loved his wife and called daily upon the name of the Lord.

When Lamech the Faithful was gifted by God a son, the baby was identical to the Shining Ones: a shimmering, pale boy with red hair who glistened as rays of sun lighting upon a basket of diamonds. Praying through moments of doubt, and fearing that a Watcher had beguiled or abused his wife, this Lamech trusted against hope that the lad was his.

And the lad *was* his. The Lord had caused the baby to appear in that likeness by His very own doing. And not just this, but He instructed an angel to whisper news of Lamech bringing a Shining One into the world.

Given the hearts of men and the quick tongues of women, the news spread that the lecher and philanderer, Lamech the Untrue, must have lain with the daughter of an angel, or let a Watcher enjoy one of his wives.

Rumors rush as the wind o'er a field of barley, and carry light and swift as the fluff of cotton. The public mixed the two Lamechs, having no occasion for surprise at an otherworldly extension in the fold of the household of Cain – for there were many – and gave the matter no further thought or consideration.

Thus was the household of Lamech the Good left unencumbered to raise their very mortal, but very special, son. The babe spoke his first words less than a week after birth's first cry, the young prophet singing praises of God and warnings to Man.

And Lamech called the child Noah.

***

God, having quietly protected from youth His appointed messenger, made a second discreet work amongst men.

A hermit, lame, with crooked back and knobbed, contorted knuckles, began to surface where the influential and the powerful amongst men trafficked. His mission was singular: to teach men about the importance of nations and the separation of powers.

The complexity of the task was high, for the whole of the earth was governed by a central government divided, like unto a single pie, into sections or slices of administrations, numbering just ten. To whomever would lend him ear and pedestal he would preach, saying that men should draw up natural boundaries and separate themselves. No longer should they live stacked as fish in great, dense cities. Rather, families should spread out into small rural communities.

His teachings were foreign to the minds of his hearers, most of whom only knew living in great megalopolises with ease of drink, commerce, revelry, and rioting ever available for the indulging. Opposite of these were those who favored the other extreme. The hermit encountered many like him who advocated living solitary lives, having neither connection, root, nor neighbor. He labored to teach men to dismiss the excesses of each approach, considering the middle ground and the concept of small towns or villages.

Sovereignty.
Separation.
Protection of freedom.

Again and again the hermit preached, a primitive prophet begging the distracted and the dumbed-down to understand that fish must not be kept in one basket, neither sheep in one fold, lest the wolf come and eat all of them, sparing not, ending the species.

While Noah was young, being reared quietly, a wee sprig of a strong plant yet to emerge from the shadows, his forerunner begged, persuaded, and did all to teach men.

But alas, before countries were, patriots were not found, and all were one tongue and one collective flock: lambs for the slaughtering, crying back at the hermit that the sum of life was to eat, to drink, and to be merry.

Chapter 24
The Owl and the Raven

Morgaine, already the height of a tall warrior at seven, was persistent in her inquiry of her foster-father and apparent sovereign (she giggled in unbelief at the account of the bombastic wiles of her ever companion, thinking, *How can a jester be a king?*), refusing to do her chores or to order their tiny home.

"Dust gathers quickly in a hut hewn of rock, daughter. And your bedding, if not soon changed, may cause the bedframe to rust, else invite the rats in."

"You're not my father!" The common refrain. "Besides, our home is clean – ever always so clean that it offends vermin, and a visitor could eat from the floor!"

Fists clenched, arms stiff as logs at her side, the child stormed from the cottage and climbed angrily to the summit of the hollow mount that contained their home, pelting the Puck with one more hiss of "You're not my father!" for good measure.

Gwyn left the lass to her tantrum for a few minutes, then hastened to follow, for they did have a visitor coming whose appearance might frighten the maiden.

Straight beneath the high sun, only the outline of whatever circled above could be seen; large wings, flapping, circling. Great hind legs and the silhouette of hooves, circling. The size of the shadow increasing, its caster moving in closer. Morgaine wondered, *Am I now the fish?* The head of it was of no beast, nor a fowl of the air, for the shadow did outline hair, and at that the hair of woman. Circling.

Gwyn presently joined Morgaine and whatever circled them, blocking the sun with its descending presence.

"Answers come with time and patience, daughter, not in accord to the whims and insatiable curiosity of a child. We have exercised your mind; now we begin to train your body."

As it – rather, *she* – came into view, the shadow was resorbed by the true: the stunning Huntress was over them directly, then alighting, with elegance and grandeur, in the midst of the Faerie King and the goddess Morrigan.

"Your hair is just as mine." Lilith omitted introduction. "Although mine once became as wool, but that is not a tale for a child."

The gold in Morgaine's eyes flared as she glared. She feared nothing, including the part-bird, part-cow, part-woman thing making pejorative accusation against her maturity – for after all, she was already *seven*.

"And I am one thousand and three and seventy, Raven." Lilith played with the girl's hair, ordering it, revealing a beautiful visage under the dishevelment of a young one who had spent her life in rock and wood.

"How did you hear my thoughts?" Morgaine was irritated but fascinated by the trick, and even more fascinated by how good it felt to have another female, *if that was what the owl-creature was*, touch her hair.

Lilith did more, taking Morgaine's hand and guiding her down the crag, away from the elf, away from men, away from the world. More mothering and fellowship there occurred in two minutes than had happened for the sum of Morgaine's seven years, or Lilith's ten centuries.

"A witch is a female offspring of the angels, whom men will come to call 'daughters of devils,' and not altogether falsely. They are born with unique powers. Amongst these are the ability to move objects, discern thoughts, control the mists, divine the future, and such. A Primal Witch is one who is directly born of a Watcher, or of the Most Elect Hosts of Heaven, and by a daughter of humanity's first parents, for in the beginning He made them male and female." Lilith here stopped short of giving greater detail.

"You are a better teacher than my father!" Morgaine threw her voice, ensuring that the unwanted male, who had now joined them, could hear the comparative insult. He laughed.

Lilith took Morgaine's face in her hands, declaring, "Of course I am."

He laughed again, his only counter. "I leave you ladies to it." And with a bow and twist, he, in his accustomed manner, vanished.

"The Elven Lord did not speak amiss, for I am here to train you in combat, not history or philosophy. Though I think you will be as natural at the former as the latter, needing very little advice from this 'part cow.'"

"I am sorry."

"Never put another down to elevate thyself."

"You said 'no philosophy,' mistress." Morgaine was already besting the Owl, just as she had the Puck for as long as she could remember.

Lilith allowed one fang to be unsheathed: a half-smile for her pupil, who equally amazed the Ancient Sorceress. "Have you a weapon?"

After her defeat of Uriel, Lilith, who was already an invincible, undefeated combatant with her hands and fangs, had decided to *improve* herself by adding a weapon. From the broken fragment of Uriel's famous blade, she had compelled the cyclops Arges, the sole survivor of the slaughter upon the shores of the Euphrates, to fashion her a long weapon. Arges was as the blacksmith to the gods, having made a trident for Poseidon and a winged helm for the hero Hermes.

Lilith had guided the design, instructing him to make a spike, or battle-dirk, rather than a hilted sword. The first of its kind, it was one continuous shaft thinning to a spike on both ends. In the place of the hilt was another blade, shaped as a wide crescent moon. A braid of leather beneath the crescent moon and another towards the top of the instrument allowed the wielder to hold the device at either, or both, ends effectively.

"I'm but a child," Morgaine said, showing her unarmed, empty hands.

Knowing that the remnant of Uriel's sword was wrapped, concealed or even buried somewhere in or near the cottage, Lilith concluded that Gwyn had not repaired or refashioned it, at least not yet. "Well, here then is the standard sword of the Olympians, one I acquired in a—" Lilith struggled to give the lass overt details about bloodshed so young. "A contest."

Morgaine brandished the steel, light and easy to swoosh. "Did the original owner survive the match?"

Full-fanged laughter ensued as Lilith acquiesced to the fact that the child was no child. "He did not."

And thus did the Owl begin to train the Raven; the battle-dirk versus the sword.

A routine, a ritual of training and companionship, began. The girl and the woman allowed themselves one hour of time *as women*, as mother and daughter, and over time, as peers or friends. Then for three hours, brutal combat would ensue.

Plant and herbal lore, the movement of the luminaries, the doctrines of the astral dragons, mind sciences, theology, philosophy. Tea, customs and styles of dress, how to plait and present the hair.

Then on to the twenty-thousand ways to kill a man, a giant, or a winged thing.

The ritual continued, six days a week, for seven years. Lilith never lodged with the unlikely family, retreating to her own place, her forest, at session's end. She cherished this time, cautiously.

Morgaine's footwork was better than Lilith's – *and how can a skill be better than perfect?*

In strength, Morgaine won also.

In swordplay, Morgaine.

In defense, Morgaine.

In cunning, Lilith yet had the advantage. But such would surely be supplanted by reason of time and experience.

Careful to not bring injury or harm to the child, when Morgaine was ten, Lilith executed the maneuver by which she would attack the neck (only with neither bite nor puncture), then catch the shoulder at the socket from the side. This was the move that accompanied dismemberment of scores of the Owl's foes.

Morgaine, feeling the pressure of her shoulder being contorted and moved unnaturally, wanting to separate from the socket that housed it, simply clasped her hands, using the free arm to form a ring with the first, the leverage putting the shoulder in its proper place, the downward motion breaking Lilith's grasp. Reflexively and in the same motion, Morgaine reversed the move and, popping her hip into Lilith's midsection, violently flipped her teacher to the soil.

The child rose and recoiled, respectfully, and also with some fear of rapid recompense.

Instead, the air felt as though time itself had stopped. The sun and the moon looked down, frozen in disbelief, pausing their courses. The birds likewise took note of the moment, stilling their songs.

Aside from melee's nicks and scratches, or the odd giant bruising her during its plummet of death, Lilith had never suffered any real damage in combat aside from Uriel's one cut. And that had been more entertaining than concerning. But now she had truly been bested. Her offense had been countered with defense, speed, quick wittedness, and a painful finishing maneuver.

A ten-year-old had flung the god-killer to the ground as if she were a sack of small potatoes.

Chapter 25
The Passing of Eve

Adam died. The breath that animated him did the Father draw back unto Himself.

To Tartarus did the faithful angels conduct Adam's soul, there to rest in bliss, dreaming of his garden: a warm and happy slumber, awaiting a new body with which to one day frolic with bears, wrestle bison, and hold his wife in a new Paradise upon a restored Earth.

But Eve lived longer, made to see the dawn of Day Two of humanity; a grieving widow left to witness the fall of Atlantis without her mate. Aged, melancholy to her core, she was a ghost whose fount of tears had dried, having no more water after a thousand years of error, tragedy, murder, and loss.

She was saved through childbearing, just as God had declared. But the pains of labor that drove Eve's faith to the Lord was the birth of the world, for she was its mother, for better and for worse, and a rebellious and disobedient child it was.

Daily she prayed that flawed men would overcome their flesh, remember the Most High, regard the poor, and do better. Daily, He who hears prayers was silent. Men were left to their own free will, and with it chose self-destruction.

In the eleven hundred and eightieth year, Eve, empty of tears and out of prayers, fell sick and was nigh unto death.

***

Morgaine was fourteen years old that year, and still following the daily routine with her friend and only mother she had ever known.

As iron sharpens iron, Lilith, whose readiness and intensity increased with every lesson, never allowed Morgaine to throw her again. The incident was singular, and both participants pointed back to it as a day that would be revisited when the battle was real, and not for tutoring.

At fourteen, Morgaine was taller than a normal man, but not as the giants or the cyclopes. Her build was slender, marble and sinew wrapped in tight, dark skin. Her hair was naturally wild but straightened, and when made to adorn herself in a gown, she was beautiful – else she had the appearance of a smudgy, muddy-kneed woodland eremite.

The Screech Owl could at least assume a brilliant radiance that exceeded her pupil's, who, lacking breasts, yet looked like a wild boy. This pleased Lilith, who swallowed daily lumps of jealousy, a mixture of gall and honey, for she loved the lass; *but why is she not serpentine, or blessed with three arms or a forked tongue?*

"Three arms would make wrestling you to the pitch much easier, Mother." The 'wild boy' could apparently read minds too, thought the 'part cow.'

"Ah, Morgaine, your natural skills are remarkable." Lilith noted that she must now shield her thoughts, lest her young student see the life of rape and brutality that had made her. "And soon you will need me not. This is but one example of why the life of a witch must be, and shall always be, solitude."

"You would leave me!" Spittle left the girl's mouth and her breathing quickened, her heart jumping and falling, her stomach cramping.

"I have always been here, and though I know not what the future holds, I will circle in from my forest home from time to time. But understand, my Morgaine, that we will ever be hunted and hated, for we are different. Should one day come when I see you no more, I may be engaged with winged scorpions, or in the jowls of three-headed dogs. The world is filled with a diversity of madness."

"Is that why you have invested so much time in training me?" Morgaine asked.

"In part." More use of magick to shield memory's pain. "There is an old foe, and we thought perhaps you and I could one day work together to defeat, perchance to even kill him."

"What does it mean to kill one of us?" The question of the Age surfaced again, this time from the teen witch. "And when my parent died, where did she go?"

"Ah, your mother went to rest in glory, safe and sound in a gilded hall within Tartarus, to be certain." Lilith gave an easy answer to a layered question.

"No, not my mortal mother. I know nothing of her save that she was a princess. I refer to my parent, to the nurse that raised me."

"As I have said oft afore, daughter," the elf grumped, "when killed by the bear, her spirit returned to Olympus, there to rest among her people."

Morgaine's examination changed direction. "If Lilith has ever been my guardian, traversing the heavens, ensuring that I grew safe and sound in the solitude of our hidden abode, how did she not see the bear and rend it in twain ere it undid my nurse-mother?"

"Even the most watchful owl sees not all. Even a powerful Seer is subject to sleep, and to misfortune," Lilith replied, her answer grave and apologetic. "What brings you into the ladies' circle?" A subject change. An audience change.

Concerning importance and presence in Morgaine's life, Lilith had increased, the Fae King diminished. She adored him, but her enamor with having some form of a mother, and another woman in her life, had caused the lass's relationship with Gwyn to wither upon the vine, starved of affection, attention, and cultivation.

Full of grace and understanding, he had concluded that all girls of this age forsake time with their fathers. The elf was a complicated person with a complicated life, and though he missed Morgaine grievously, there were a myriad of other intrigues, conspiracies and adventures that the discarded imp could hurl himself into. But on this day he had manifested, finding the two warriors training near a brook, the rush of the stream and hollow calmness of the winds adding a solemnity to his appearance.

Following his foster-daughter's long embrace, the elf made use of the loud backdrop, taking the Owl aside, tidings given at a murmur.

"Your other foe of old is at the grave's door, knocking. Another fortnight she will not see." The Fae beseeched Lilith that she show mercy, reduce the lifelong verdict to a long probation, and allow Eve to see her grandchild but once before dying.

"The testimony of Eileithyia died when we slew her." Gwyn reminded Lilith that the 'bear' story would allow Morgaine to go through life never knowing that Eve had been kept from her, and she from Eve, by Lilith's vengeful design. A plentitude of other stories could be authored as to why it was too dangerous for Eve to meet the exiled daughter of Awan without revealing the Screech Owl's hand in the separation. Eve would not live forever, and Morgaine's long life had just begun; the Fae King and the Owl had been hoping to wait it out, to lie through it, and come through the matter with the First Mother gone and without the new Primal Witch hating them.

Lilith trusted that Gwyn could manage and manipulate the discourse enough to avoid calamity, and although not enamored with what was about to be, agreed to ending the banishment. A suspension of malice, that Eve might look upon Awan and Luluwa once more, beholding them in the visage of Morgaine.

***

Morgaine instantly missed Lilith, her mind recollecting their final conversation again and again, as if the conversation was pinned to a waterwheel. *The solitude of a witch. Will I see her again?* But the Raven was also excited, for she had never traveled beyond the rocks and forest that contained her home.

Gwyn knew that questions would now fall heavy and without ceasing, as one of the waterfalls that garnished their special lands. Wanting very much to listen to what Eve or surrounding family and friends might say *before* weaving tales of partial truths and dangerous lies, the Fae King required that the fourteen-year-old quell her curiosity until after Eve passed. She would fade soon, he told her, and was the most famous of all living (for Enoch was raptured and Noah blended and concealed amongst the Shining Ones, his ministry not yet initiated by the Lord), and an old friend of his besides. Gwyn feigned sorrow and distress, not speaking on anything of substance during the long journey.

***

God required that the hermit also attend the passing of Eve. The crippled servant of the Lord begged otherwise but could not resist the directed will of the Father, who used a whirlwind to transport the preacher, sending him from the south (where he had been pleading with men to break from the ten regions and form a confederacy of small nation states) in an instant to the Cave of Treasures, where lay Eve, adorned in white vestments: a lonely, dying queen surrounded by thousands of children and children's children's children.

But not Luluwa. Not Awan. Not Awan's baby.

Then joy appeared, delivered ironically by the very horned and hooved things that Eve, above all things, loathed. She was too sick to care, but within her brilliant mind the irony was not lost on the failing sovereign.

The mob forbade the hermit, who was a dozen or more rings of onlookers removed, from seeing the Elect Lady at first. Michael and Gabriel presided over the scene and, obeying God's command, parted the masses.

"I see that Providence hath yielded many peculiar witnesses on this day." The Archangel Gabriel guided the hermit to Eve's bedside, where Morgaine already knelt, hugging her *new* grandmother.

Through smothering curtains of black hair, the happy, dying mother captured a glimpse of the hooded guest, watching the meeting and crying happy tears, thanking a merciful God for granting the dying wishes of a precious soul.

"Who are you?" she managed.

"Just an old servant come to see you, my lady," he said.

The eyes were familiar, but Eve could not recall who he was, and was too old, too near death, and too happy to care. Instead, not concerned whatsoever that she would soon pass away, she did what all grandmothers do. Sitting straight up in bed with miraculous verve, she showed off her grandchild.

"I present my favorite granddaughter."

A chorus of thousands of spurned offspring trumpeted their protests, but Eve cared not, for the lot of them had gone whoring with fallen angels.

The hermit smiled, for Eve's moment of proud joy filled the heart of any who truly cared for her. Practicing good manners, the lame hermit labored, removing his hood, then labored further, kneeling with knees past usefulness and a back which bent the wrong way. He took the hands of Morgaine into his – she, perceiving him to be gentle and polite, consented to the same – and looked upon her.

Eve introduced her granddaughter to the hermit, uttering what would be her final words. "Meet my new Watcher. Is she not an angel?"

Saying this, the Mother of all the Living passed into sleep, joining her one true love in Tartarus, her pain and remorse for the Fall having ended.

In that very moment, the love Uriel had had for Eve which had transferred to Awan now likewise but with triple intensity did fix upon Morgaine…

Chapter 26
The Wages of Plotting

"Again, the devil taketh Him up into an exceeding high mountain, and sheweth him all the kingdoms of the world, and the glory of them;

And saith unto him, All these things will I give thee, if thou wilt fall down and worship me."

Matthew 4:19

God commanded Uriel to make visitation upon Eve, that he might be punished for his contributions to her sorrow and find continued repentance through burying the woman the Lord had trusted him to protect.

Gwyn found opportunity in Eve's passing to pry Morgaine from Lilith's ever-seeing eyes, hoping Eve would reveal that Lilith had kept Morgaine from her grandmother, from her family. In learning that she had been needlessly abandoned to be reared by elves and monsters, Morgaine would be filled with rage and vengeance towards Lilith.

Lilith had trained Morgaine to defeat Azazel. But Gwyn had manipulated Lilith into training Morgaine to defeat… Lilith.

Eve, soon after being forbidden from approaching her grandchild, had made this arrangement. For the Bards do record Gwyn as Gwyn ap Nudd, which is by translation The Shining One, son of Nodens, which is by translation The Shining One, son of Poseidon.

Gwyn did slay his own sister, the goddess of all midwives and nursemaids, that she would not warn the maiden of the scheme, for Eileithyia did fear the terror of Lilith over all things, including the Watchers. And Eve and Poseidon were friends.

But it was not the will of God that Uriel and Morgaine would meet that day. Neither did Gwyn recognize the man – only that his foster-daughter was instantly in love, and that the power and persuasion of the crippled monk was observably not from the realm of mortals.

There are plots atop plots undermined by machinations, layered with conspiracies. I know what spirit works behind all of this, for I too am fostered.

***

The elf did not have to quest far to discover his real father, who presently looked down from Mount Hermon, beaming with pride over the chaos and madness that was the world of his angels.

Thousands of heavenly beings never met him, nor directly bowed the knee to follow him. Rather they followed his patterns, his way. Neither was he amongst those who made solemn pact to go in unto the daughters of men, for he was separate, elevated, and above that plot.

But the delicious fruits of it he savored. Most of his days were spent not interacting directly with men, whom he viewed as apes, or rats, or ants, but in heaven, alongside the Counsel of the Elect, accusing the apes, rats, and ants, crying out that there was nothing in them that merited inheritance, neither salvation.

But for Eve's death, and for the coming together of Uriel and the new witch, who would surely produce sons that could at last contain, if not defeat, his estranged bride, the Cherub relished the visit. And scoffed at the visitor.

Gwyn: white, shining, light. A curious name for a creature with red skin, red eyes, and the short black horns of a stag.

A curious name for the son of the son of darkness.

"Arddu." Gwyn called his father by his personal name, in the most ancient tongue. "Lucifer. You are behind the union of the hermit and my Raven, aren't you?"

"I don't control the will of others, son. I just nudge them. A master potter working with wet, unmolded clay."

"To what end!" He who was master of riddles and lessons wrapped in jest had not the stomach for either. "Lilith will surely add me to the stack of green vapor piled in caverns and canyons and abandoned huts the world over! And worse." Gwyn truly possessed a father's love for Morgaine, and he was fond of Lilith as well. "She is fourteen, the maiden becoming of age to be a—"

"A mother," Arddu interrupted. "That is her purpose, and the sons of Uriel and the progeny of Adam and Eve will be my greatest creations. One of them surely will rise up and put the world aright, defeating the Seed of the Woman."

The prophecy.

All the manipulations of the Devil ever circle back to the simplicity of the *Seed War*. The war for possession of the Earth. Man had done a wonderful job abdicating their rightful place as heirs and agency of rule of their own accord. But Lucifer was not satisfied, and harkened unto the words of his maker. Some form of savior was coming, and an anti-savior must be ready both to rule and to carry out the full and total corruption of the seed of men.

Only then could the prophecy be thwarted and the Devil reign fully and freely as God.

The secondary and tertiary meddling of the gods was nothing but crooked paths to be trodden along the dark journey to this evil end.

"And if Morgaine dies in giving you these 'seeds?'" Gwyn, a great warrior in his own right, approached Lucifer, fists engaged.

"Then you will be compensated. Did not Adam offer you a kingdom for your part in this saga?"

The Accuser accused truly. For Adam and Eve had promised the elf a home for his kind, similar to the realm of Morgaine, where no men and few gods had trodden. And Poseidon likewise had blessed the transaction.

Trick Lilith to train Morgaine, earn a kingdom for his kind – his mischievous but nice, good people. His *Fair Folk*.

"Whether the sons of Uriel destroy Morgaine exiting the womb or not, I will expand your lands to the sides of the north, for I know they are now every bit your home. I do this in barter for your ongoing efforts to bring the little white screech owl to submission!"

These lands were actually Satan's to give. The First Family had been given the earth, and the dominion and rule thereof. When they rebelled from the one who deeded them the land, the earth itself became forfeit, and the Devil and his angels ruled, claims of dirt by mortals notwithstanding.

The Elf King was a complicated man, with complicated needs. The fists relaxed. "What would you have me do next?"

Lucifer clutched the shoulder clasp of the Puck's plaid, violently jerking him to within a dandelion's whisper of his mouth. "Find the God-damned cage!"

Gwyn nodded, removed the Cherub's grasp from his garb, and backed away several paces, yet facing his father.

"Lilith will simply kill me anyway," he concluded, agreeing to the Devil's bargain.

"Tell her the truth about your mother, *faerie*. It is inconceivable that she would abort you a second time, Shining O—"

But the elf had vanished, using his power to become light, then disappear, before Satan finished uttering the discourse's final offense.

Chapter 27
A Short Marriage to a Tall Girl

The hermit called himself Trugaredd, which is, by interpretation, in the oldest tongue *Mercy*, and he did love Morgaine.

And Morgaine, equally smitten, forgetting her senses, misplacing her judgement and shelving for a time her ability to discern the thoughts and passions of others, fell deeply and instantly in love with the hermit.

There was something overwhelmingly *familiar* about him, causing her to yearn for his protection (though she was whole, and he maimed), for his guidance (though in acumen she was his equal), and above all, his approval.

Trugaredd explained that God had called him to have no permanent dwelling, rather to traverse the earth, warning and teaching men. He was a traveler.

She had never been... *anywhere.*

For shame, and not wanting to lose the one upon whom he was fixated, Trugaredd – true to form – told compounding lies to his love.

Having no shame, and little history, Morgaine found she would rather be impaled by a thousand spears or stung by five thousand hornets than to ever be dishonest or untrue to her mate. She disclosed that she was a witch, from the start.

At this time, there was no organized religion nominated as *witchcraft*. It was a born condition, not a worldview. She was of otherworldly origins on her father's side and of ancient, primal blood on her mother's. And she informed him of her powers, her rearing by a red-skinned elf and a flying cow-owl, making it fully known that she had no idea what it meant to be amongst men, *or how to be a woman.*

A hundred opportunities presented themselves for the hermit to likewise be honest, for forthrightness and truth, which are the foundation stones of actual love. But his love for Morgaine was unnatural. He was a guardian, but more a possessor. A possessor of the worst sort: kind, romantic, and loving.

When brutish, violent, and hateful men seek to possess women, they are easy to identify, easy to flee. But Trugaredd was gentle, attentive, warm, humorous, playful, and nice. These attributes did not offset the fact that she was not his for the wanting, and justifying a horrible thing because one serves tea or holds the door can be more sinister than the backhand of a rogue.

And, certainly, more damaging.

Not only was Morgaine her mother, and her mother's mother, but she was the first person to actually *listen to and agree with him* in fourteen long years. A man heard by his wife lives full of joy, for does not every man want to impress his damsel in arms, and in knowledge?

The concept of nationhood and its paramount significance for the hope of liberty and survival – *she understood and was so intrigued by, that she promised to become the Goddess of Sovereignty and Patriotism!*

The God who was above all gods – *Morgaine believed! And feared the One who made Leviathan by His Word, and painted the heavens with His fingertips!*

The life of Trugaredd and Morgaine was very simple. He would preach God and Nation in tavern, in square, to whatever small gathering would hear him. The crowd would mock and reject him. His new young wife attended each sermon, hanging on his every word, drinking in his message, loving him more each day.

At night they would make passionate love.

Early in the morning they would depart, looking for the next opportunity to witness.

In this regard, the hermit would represent God publicly, loudly doing good, then at night practice the very act preached against. Each night, at the very instant and moment after the swell of his passion had reached climax – *the small window in time where men are honest, vulnerable, and receptive* – he would audibly hear the voice of God imploring him to 'Stop this! Stop this now!' or some nights to 'Come home!' Forcing himself to ignore God and conscience, he would turn away, cuddling his Raven in post-lovemaking bliss.

As afore, the former Fire Serpent could not outsmart or outrace his sins. They would seek him out and openly show him his folly – the folly of a growing belly in a wife who may burst asunder when a sin against nature exits her womb.

Six months after their whirlwind of travel and daily lovemaking, Morgaine was with child, the fallen angel's nightmare to renew.

When Trugaredd would stoop to wash his face in a basin, the water would turn to blood, Awan's blood, and the horrific imagery of her passing became a mirror for his remembrance. When quiet, he heard her cries. With eyes closed, he would see her. And see *it*. The incident that had so damaged and changed him, yet still not enough to change his nature or rehabilitate the rebellion within.

This will be the same again. I have murdered my love. My phallus is a false god, bringing only death and not life, my lust more fearsome than Lilith's talons.

But Morgaine's pregnancy was **not** the same as Awan's. For the girl, now fifteen, grew to accommodate the ginormous life gestating within. Not outwardly, but up. Morgaine grew taller, her bone structure changing, elongating, becoming something new the moment her pregnant body started to show.

And taller.

And taller.

Selfish Trugaredd found transitory exhilaration that she would not perish in birthing (for the titaness before him could suffer the birth of three large giants with no more discomfort than the lion when he frees a thistle from his paw), then, reckoning with the new reality, became instantly forlorn that it would be impossible to kiss, let alone make love to a woman that now stood taller than the old oaks, whose tall legs disappeared into the clouds.

Pregnancy had also caused the otherworldly lass to mature into her actual self. The Morgaine whom Gwyn had reared, Lilith trained, and Uriel loved was no more; the Goddess Morrigan was born.

Two hundred and eighty cubits tall she was, which is the length of four hundred and twenty boots, and shrouded in a flame like unto her father's – only her fire was gray, else black. The Morrigan's form remained as that of a woman in every respect, only black and purple feathers emerged along the edge of her forearms and her flesh was a composite of serpentine and mortal, causing her to appear as if she were adorned in a greenish-gray scaled armor, though she were naked.

Doing what any girl does in a moment of distress, Morgaine cried out for her elf. Next, she fled for the north. For her home.

***

To crawl into her modest cot, the skins and pelts that had given her warmth and escape for the sum of her life, to bury her face in her one special pillow and have a long cry, was not possible.

For the Morrigan presently knelt *around* the walled portions of the stone cottage, her knees running up against the side of the hill where the remainder of the domicile disappeared into the rock. Her house looked as a plaything, a structure built of twigs and mud and inhabited by dolls made of cloth and straw. She could not fit in four of her houses, or forty. The special pillow could only now give the relief of rest and cushion to her smallest toe.

The crying part came uncontrollably without those comforts. The pregnant colossus wept, giving her weight to the mountain, which creaked and crackled and shifted in protest.

This time when her owl manifested it looked like an actual owl – a baby owl at that.

"Such weeping is not favorable for the child, and beneath your station as a warrior. Steady. Raven. Mark your breathing."

"Children." The Morrigan sharply corrected her mentor, followed by a cold, "Triplets." The Goddess of Sovereignty summonsed strength and rose, slowly, intentionally. In anger she assumed her fighting stance, still perfect, against her now tiny adversary. "Will you abduct my three as well, Moon Goddess?"

The Raven had flown off and into the world and gathered the slander thereof. Lilith had dreaded the day, and the day was at hand.

***

"Fetch me Uriel. He will know the day and the hour when his sons perish, but be spared the seeing of it."

Michael the Archangel answered, "Yes, my Lord," enquiring nothing of the mother.

***

The sons of Uriel will reign over the Earth, and all gods and men shall bow before them. Arddu was pleased to hear of three suitors to the throne for the Anti-Messiah he envisioned, pondering how they might be joint heirs, or if needed, how the strongest might need to assassinate a rival, or two. Being not God, he knew not that each was a son, and also plotted how he might use marriage amongst them, a perpetual dynasty at his pleasure.

In his vain daydreaming, Satan likewise gave no mind to the mother carrying the unborn Nephilim.

Chapter 28
Lilith Versus the Morrigan

The Screech Owl fears nothing – including a teenaged, towering offspring of an archangel, still discovering her own powers and under the raging influence of false assumptions (and the uniquely volatile rudiments that accompany pregnancy).

"Would your foster-father, a lord just and true, ally with an abductor and killer of infants?" Lilith demanded. "In no wise!"

"Perhaps the allegiance was false and had an aim."

The Morrigan was correct. Gwyn had created the circumstances by which Lilith would raise up her own destroyer.

The veracity of Morgaine's words found their mark, registering as true. Lilith, realizing she had been made the fool, uttered weak protest. "But… we were to fight Azazel, together."

"Zeus I know of; Hera, and Poseidon too. Cronus and the chiefs of those Old Ones, who started all this cry in their chains from the abyss. Them I know. But this Azazel, famed in ancient myths for teaching women how to paint their nails and showing men use of torch and lantern, how to provide heat to hearth and home – I know nothing of him, whether or not he even is, and why I should concern myself with the matter." The giantess shrugged.

Dismissive devaluation of Lilith's enemy. Her abhorrent adversary. Her vile father. Enraged and betrayed, now Lilith, too, was ready to fight.

Morgaine's mind was shielded from Lilith's invasion, likewise Lilith's thoughts hedged as if by granite her apprentice's encroachment. Not knowing what Morgaine did nor did not know about her vagabond prophet and lover, a pebble was preferred to a boulder.

"You know nothing of Azazel? Well. What about Uriel?"

The buildup of cross words was concluded; the battle was at hand. But this was no training exercise. This was not a spar, nor a wrestling match. Lilith's battle-dirk would not be withheld at moment of contact – no more scrapes where gashes were earned.

And she had earned the first gash.

The Morrigan retained the speed of her former, more 'normal-sized' self, but had not mastered her range. Lilith fought the contest from the air, swirling and twirling, performing aerial somersaults just out of the reach of her opponent's punches and swipes.

Morgaine having no weapon, the scene was as a naked child running to and fro in the field, chasing fireflies. But this firefly, finding Morgaine exhausted, turned hornet and attacked. Waiting for a final, looping and now lazy swing, the Screech Owl went into and not away from the strike. Evading the danger, she slashed Morgaine on the right side, where the neck meets the inside of the shoulder. Not waiting idly to admire her cut, the Primal Witch flew into the heavens, leagues away from the wounded Raven below.

The battle-dirk, forged of her own father's sword, opened the lass as a fount, dyeing the rocky gray terrain with bright, fresh blood. Morgaine looked at the wound, thinking quickly how she might seal it, and which herbs would most rapidly promote healing. *Just so long as I don't bleed out while evaluating picking roots and berries!* She laughed aloud. One cut would not a titan fell.

At this moment did the Morrigan discover her ability to control weather, in the age before weather was…

Lilith was soaring through the mists, sailing as a sleek barge at great speed. Then the mists transformed into heavy clouds, a thunderstorm that surrounded her, arresting her flight. The enchantment filled her body with enough lightning to cook ten oxen.

Pointing to the heavens where the witch toiled with the cloud, Morgaine made a simple, downward flick, causing the Owl to plummet at great speed in concert with the gesture, slammed hard to the rocky earth by her pupil's magick.

The first Fallen One had fallen. Was cast down.

A cloud of dust billowed high, then – silence...

Silence. But no green gooey vapor, nor an apparition wailing, bemoaning its end o'er the place of its death. Lilith was not vanquished, only angered.

Moving the rubble and heaps of dirt and branches off her wings and hooves, Lilith ascended from the crater caused by her violent fall. Eyes filled with madness, the furious Owl hissed, "You command the mists, I the fowls of the air!"

Authoritative, short phrases caused a swarm of owls to appear, numberless, as locusts, all of them fixed on the gargantuan head of the Morrigan. They pecked, clawed and harassed.

The titaness remained calm, fending them off and swooping them away as she could, but they were blinding, a blizzard of white feathers and red eyes. As they pecked and clawed, Lilith hacked and slashed.

The bottom front of the right knee first; the back of the left heel to follow. Rendered immobile, the goddess lunged, lost her balance, then collapsed upon her face, her palms absorbing most of the fall. The owls scattered as dust from a beaten carpet.

Where Lilith had caused a crater, Morgaine's plunge opened a gulley, a newly formed long canyon in the Earth. Water soon found the trench, covering the defeated warrior in a mask of muddy blood.

"At least your breasts are now covered," Lilith, expelling her rage and coming back into her right mind, mused. "We now own one victory apiece. May there never be a third contest." The Screech Owl labored to roll the felled oak onto her back so that she would not drown in the muck and shame.

"Victory is yours," Morgaine declared aloud, but in her heart she vowed, *I will never be defeated again, until the Creator Himself adjudicates me.* "Why do you not kill me, assuring your place of primacy over the Ages to Come?"

"Because—" Lilith struck Morgaine with closed fist upon the nose. Some residual rage lingered. "I," another punch, "do not," a third, "kill," a fourth blow, "children!"

The Morrigan's head was too large, and too thick, to be naught but insulted by the strokes, but the point was made.

Lilith rummaged the stone cottage for what might be used for dressing, gathered herbs to slow the blood and calm the nerves without harming the babies, then left, a visage of pride, hurt, and anger. "Grandmother is a liar!"

Morgaine, in a fit of emotion and not knowing what to believe, what to say, or what to do, shook her fist in the air, declaring, "No. You are wrong! You are wrong! I am Grandmother's Watcher!"

Alone, bleeding, she limped but mostly crawled into the wood, using ancient trees as her only shelter, for neither cave nor castle could house her. Her body forced her to shut down for the sake of her three sons, growing within. *The life of a witch is solitary,* she remembered, before pain, blood loss, and distress brought deep sleep.

Chapter 29
Of Schemes and Plots of Freakish Monsters and Crossbreeds of the Fall of Atlantis

Morgaine was alone.

Gabriel and Michael provided an involuntary escort of her hermit to the Third Heaven; the Faerie King was about his 'real' father's business, questing to propitiate the Devil's bargain. He traversed the land, searching for the Owl's lost cage. Satan wanted his wife recaptured or worse, believing that she alone could contend with the great gods that grew within the titanic lass.

But the keepers of the relic, the Order of the Dragon, who served the same master but with contrary objectives, had hidden it well.

When performing public rites, they worshipped Lilith, the Moon Goddess, giving offerings that she might spare the children. Privily, she was a thorn in their collective sides, and they prayed that she would spare them that they might continue to *spare not the children.*

Evil is a tricky enterprise. For they also very much needed her alive, and, on occasion, active. The occasional sighting of the Screech Owl, the real witness of terror, fueled by rumor, was a cloak for their deeds. Deities in this Age were worshipped by sight, not by faith. Should she go unseen for long years, should giants not fall to her in the field, an actual myth she would be. And actual myths don't steal children in the night, nor leave strange markings on mutilated animals.

If she were dead, or captured, fewer of their ranks would fall. But the prospect of continued iniquity outweighed the risk of some loss, for each priest, in the end, cared only for himself and his impunity to exercise his dark desires.

The Devil, understanding that God, who is longsuffering, was engaged in a slow, long contest, mirrored his Adversary. Eve had perished. The Seed of the Woman was not, from all that Satan could observe, a prophecy of a direct child from the First Mother. Therefore, he concluded, the Messiah rather must come from *her line*. Though the life is in the blood, and the blood is provided by the father, somehow – by some miracle – a maiden must be with child, lest the line was stamped out.

The Watchers had mocked this miracle prior to its manifestation by producing 'heavenly babies,' but Satan knew that what must come would not be by that means; not unholy, not driven by fornication and carnality and forbidden offenses. Knowing not what the Most High would do, the serpent continued to be haunted by the prophecy. He, as the hydra, possessed many heads, many plans, and many schemes to thwart the Creator.

And to all appearances, his policies were winning; none more so than the policy of simply encouraging divisiveness amongst the remnant of men, and the subtle suggestion to breed them out of existence (with the hope that the sons of Uriel would have the power and resolve to order the chaos of the resulting world of gods and monsters). For Eve had indeed perished, and her line, which is the line of all humanity, was in dread crisis.

But Lilith, the Bride of the Devil, saved babies. Mortal babies, born of mortal parents.

The Order of the Dragon robbed infants of their essence and then ritually murdered them. For their ministry of madness to tarry, she must not again be caged, or killed outright. The policy of ending the line of Eve was good for angels, bad for men – even for this collective of lewd criminals. If all the sheep are slaughtered, what role remains for the hireling?

Thus did the learners and keepers of the Occult Sciences study other abominations, hoping to restore more noble, balanced-thinking gods. Experimenting with the ghostly remnants of Lilith's kills, devising ways to allow their essence to possess men and copulate with unwilling women, creating unholy lives of their own.

For Man is creative, being like unto his Creator. And even evil men will persevere towards the survival of their kind.

They sought the restoration of venerating the act as a 'Sacred Marriage,' and not a wanton, crazed obsession. The quantity and the matching were the quandaries, not the untoward deed itself. For that which is sacred must be scarce, not practiced in the open of the day. Arcane and not mundane.

They believed in, and worked for, a ruling class of gods who would marry extraordinary wives, specially selected, and fashion (and protect) a bloodline to rule over men. These, in the mind of the Order of the Dragon, would always be, of course, of the stock of Cain. Never Seth. After establishing the line, the god-men would reproduce after their kind and be as the Shining Ones, immortal but normal-looking, thereafter only rarely introducing angelic siring into the family tree.

The madness of angels diluting the female population to zero by means of a myriad of strange mixtures would lead to a world of barren donkeys, they feared, and ultimately the end of life itself. Thus were the factions of devil-worshippers contentious, disagreeing about how best to ransack and usurp God's creation and deceive, control and murder men.

The Olympians, not retaining in their great wisdom the knowledge of a 'devil', likewise dealt with their mounting and manifold dilemmas. For utopia hardly endures when scores of women die giving birth to giants – giants who eat the men, the children, and each other. Flying machines and a patchwork of roads that allow an erudite traveler to find his destination using the stars above and grid below have no use for those born without functioning eyes, or with thirty eyes but no feet.

And for God and the faithful courts of heaven, there too was work rumored and whispered: the wheat to be sorted from the chaff.

Whisper gave way to discourse. God was so vexed that He declared, full of sorrow, rage, and feeling, to the Powers,

Principalities, Dominions, Thrones, Cherubs, and Seraphim, that the Three Who Is One regretted making a being like unto Himself, and that the relationship between the Creator and His special creation had failed. Was woefully broken.

Yet for His great love with which He loved them, the Lord recovered His resolve, having known from the foundation of the world that He Himself would atone for their rebellion, and defeat death itself.

Four hundred years before calling Noah and setting him apart to preach unto a dying world, God made His decree in heaven, telling its Hosts that Atlantis would fall…

Chapter 30
What the Devil Means for Evil God Uses for Good

"¹⁴ They are dead, they shall not live; they are deceased, they shall not rise: therefore hast thou visited and destroyed them, and made all their memory to perish."

Isaiah 24:16

On the Fourth Day of Creation, God spoke into existence all the angels, along with their stars. Only the Lord knows their number, for to men they are as countless as grains of sand. Yet He knows each of their names, their qualities, the courses of their stars, and the type of celestial body they inhabit.

They were allowed both to witness and participate in the garnishing of the creation, seeing the Earth positioned and settled upon its pillars, shouting for joy at the marvels of the Earth, the sky, and the wonders of the Deep.

In the Second Heaven were multitudes of them placed, running circuits day by day, telling the story of the Son of God with their luminary forms. Still ten thousand thousand more were given dwelling above the circle of the Earth, in the Third Heaven, which has seven stories, and is also the location of the throne of the Most High.

Twelve is the number of governance, and twelve times twelve is one hundred and forty-four thousand. This is the number of the Kingdom of Heaven, and the number of mansions within the City of God, the capital of creation, the inheritance of angels from which their princes were to serve and support men, whose inheritance was the Earth.

And from the one hundred and forty-four thousand were the most excellent commissioned as Watchers, to be in the world of men, quiet and stoic amongst them, as Holy Ones, to help, guard and guide. But of these, two hundred and twelve lusted after the most peculiar and precious treasure in heaven, or in earth, or below the earth. The thirteenth led them, and he was called Azazel.

And the things that were begotten of the lust of the Watchers did God hate. The nature of the aversion was as when a mother-in-law loathes the husband of her daughter, and simply acts as if he doesn't exist. Dead to her, though he liveth, he is nothing – a canker, a blemish, there but not to be acknowledged, and never spoken of. He is regarded as worse than an enemy, for an enemy is given respect and decorum – honors and rules of engagement at arms. This form of loathing considers its object unworthy of such courtesies, for it disdains consideration of him at all.

And if contact cannot be avoided, if provoked on the Holy Days, at the banquet or around the table of feasting, should the mother-in-law be forced to look upon him – or worse, dare he to speak against her – the rage is such that all flee. For her ignoring him is in earnest the storing up of wrath and when unleashed, a fire-breathing dragon is loosed to destroy him, the banquet, the hall, the honored guests, and the village that contains them...

God called all the archangels before the majesty of His seat. The Seraph surrounding the throne, singing praises of glory; the Cherub likewise worshipping with harp and stringed instrument.

The Lord spoke openly, though He knew betrayal yet lurked, even in this circle, amongst them.

"In the End of Days..." the Lord said.

The songs stopped. All listened reverently, the tone of their Maker filling them with fear.

"An evil Sovereign will rise, and free men must choose their allegiance, their faith, and the object of their love. He will be accompanied by villainous monsters, foul beasts and seductive spirits, giving the Sons of Adam a perfect contrast to God, and my ways, and the perversions thereof. For good and evil are not co-equal. Good is defined by God's truth, attributes and character. Evil is the bending of that which is good to its own aims. They are neither twins, nor a duality of forces, nor gods."

Michael had heard these things a plentitude of times, but he could tell that the build-up was hurling towards revelation.

God continued, "Thus, only to contrast the choice, which must ever accompany the liberty of men, and magnify the glory of the good, is evil allowed to long endure. Now—" God pointed to the Earth, showing them Apollos, a son of Zeus. "You see how this lad possesses destructive powers, how that his breath causes consumption and one sup from his wine hollows the throat, causing swift and gory death? The very construct of his body fashioned to annihilate, and cause pain and anguish?"

The question was not rhetorical. The patient Father gave space for response.

"Yes!" Michael was overwhelmed with understanding. "He is not random, rather designed for—"

"Apollos the Destroyer is needed for the End of Days." God stated it plainly, using a son of Zeus as a real, literal, prophetic object lesson. "Would I create something as this?"

"Never, Lord, never," Michael affirmed.

God gave him a smile that at once communicated pleasure that Michael understood His meaning without relenting His hot anger by even one degree. "Thank you, Satan. Monsters were needed for the Son of Man to vanquish, and you, my Anointed Cherub, have supplied them in droves. In the straightening of your crookedness will the nations rejoice, your evil to magnify the goodness of the Savior." For glory is the Lord's, and He will not share it with another.

It is not known whether Satan heard the derision.

"My judgement is this," the treatise continued. "The rebellious Watchers who remain: command them to return to their stars, today."

A thousand questions entered Michael's mind. He asked none, but worried after the wives and children left in a forced exodus, for some of them did have normal marriages.

"Gabriel, once the Elders of the Rebellion are removed, influence the giants, set one against the other. Stir unspeakable strife, leaving Poseidon and Zeus devastated and demoralized in a great civil war of the Nephilim."

"And Azazel as well?" Gabriel could not resist, still befuddled that the Watchers would not be put down below with the Titans.

The Lord heard Gabriel's enquiry but turned to Michael, saying, "Azazel take; fasten him to the belt of Orion, stretched out and upside down. Close one of his eyes, permanently." God did not provide details as to the means. "The other fix open, also permanently." Again, leaving the details to His angel. "Let all marvel at the fallen goat whose sins ruined the world.

"Leviathan will release the fountains of the Deep, and the guardians of the four winds will stand down. The windows of heaven will open, and… all flesh will be destroyed."

"But my sons – my love!"

"Your wings are mended, my child." God beheld Uriel holding his face, sobbing. "Your sons have no soul. Can that which is not natural ever be killed, or did it ever exist?" The Most High was as conciliatory as His righteous rage would permit. "If a child fashions a frog from clay, is it a frog?"

"What will become of them, of her?" the serpent begged.

"They will be thrown into the Lake of Fire, having no further awareness that they are, or ever were."

"All of them?"

"Aye."

Uriel moaned and wailed. Gabriel and Michael ministered to him.

"For most, the deluge will separate their animating elements, or 'spirit,' from their unholy houses of false flesh. Others will be dealt with on a more individual basis, punished on the merits of their works. Lastly, one tenth will be reserved, left to roam the face of the Earth until the End of Days. For the Savior will make a show of them, defeating them as a signature and prophecy of His coming. His power over these, who shall henceforth be called Unclean Spirits, or Demons, will validate His message and His ministry."

"How do those living down there know if they are polluted, having no soul?" Gabriel thought on the countless mixtures occurring in the mad world below.

"If a Watcher lies with a woman and the child is male, there is no soul, nothing to resurrect.

"If the male child then mates with a mortal woman and begets a male, there is nothing to resurrect.

"If a Watcher lies with a woman and the child is female, she shall not be resurrected. If a mortal male shall lie with the female offspring of the Nephilim, the child, having its father's blood, will have a soul, and be part of the resurrection.

"Thus, if a mortal man enter the bloodline, then have the progeny of the Fallen Ones hope. For the life is in the blood, and the blood comes by way of the father.

"If ten generations of Nephilim bring forth a daughter and she marries a Son of Adam, then will their son, or daughter, be mortal."

"In just a few short generations, except the genealogies be flawless, will any know what they are, who they are, or where they will go? What misery to not know!" Uriel was inconsolable. "How will you decide the one-tenth? And how long will more—" The broken archangel searched for a fitting way to describe the condition of those who would *live* yet never fully know if they were destined, without hope of retribution, for the Lake of Fire. That place of indescribable torment he himself had experienced as first-hand witness, being the chief custodian of Tartarus.

"For seven more generations will the world reap what it sowed, only now knowing openly that brimstone and annihilation, everlasting destruction, awaits. They will dwell upon the Earth, eating, drinking, and making merry, but lying down to slumber each night wondering when the end will come. The everlasting end. For these will be the generations *of the Woeful and Sorry Damned.*"

"The one-tenth remnant?" Uriel begged, beseeched, and bawled.

God said, "Your sons will not be amongst them, neither the tall maiden born of the sea."

Author Profile

Zane Newitt is an internationally-recognized Arthurian scholar, folklorist and historian born on September 3rd, 1975 in Glenwood Springs, Colorado, USA. A prolific writer, Dr. Newitt published Volume One of the epic seven-volume Arthuriad saga in 2017, with ongoing plans for short poems, spinoffs and a Morgaine cycle, the first of released in Winter 2022.

Zane is known for reviving the 'Bardic Method' - a writing style that combines epic poetry, Welsh Nationalism, folklore, theology and history in a uniquely "druidesque" blend that conceals more than it reveals, as well as containing something to inspire and offend anyone... Just as Merlin would do.

What Did You Think of
The Morgaine Cycle One Gwyliwr?

A big thank you for purchasing this book. It means a lot that you chose this book specifically from such a wide range on offer. I do hope you enjoyed it.

Book reviews are incredibly important for an author. All feedback helps them improve their writing for future projects and for developing this edition. If you are able to spare a few minutes to post a review on Amazon, that would be much appreciated.

Publisher Information

rowanvale books

Rowanvale Books provides publishing services to independent authors, writers and poets all over the globe. We deliver a personal, honest and efficient service that allows authors to see their work published, while remaining in control of the process and retaining their creativity. By making publishing services available to authors in a cost-effective and ethical way, we at Rowanvale Books hope to ensure that the local, national and international community benefits from a steady stream of good quality literature.

For more information about us, our authors or our publications, please get in touch.

www.rowanvalebooks.com
info@rowanvalebooks.com